GALADRIA : PETER HUDDLESTON & THE RITES OF PASSAGE

✳ ✳ ✳

BOOK 1

MIGUEL LOPEZ DE LEON

ISBN-10: 0692227261
ISBN-13: 9780692227268

GALADRIA : PETER HUDDLESTON & THE RITES OF PASSAGE

✳ ✳ ✳

BOOK 1

MIGUEL LOPEZ DE LEON

TABLE OF CONTENTS

Chapter 1: The Boy with the Boomerang   1

Chapter 2: Unexpected News   14

Chapter 3: Hillside Manor   28

Chapter 4: Meeting Gillian   44

Chapter 5: Negotiations   58

Chapter 6: Study, Study, Study   74

Chapter 7: Through the Looking Glass   90

Chapter 8: The Moons of Destritor   106

Chapter 9: Rune   119

Chapter 10: Soul Searching   130

Chapter 11: Baptism by Fire   133

Chapter 12: Back to Beige   156

About the Author: 161

1

THE BOY WITH THE
BOOMERANG

I guess you could say that Peter Huddleston was a peculiar boy. That's what almost everyone he knew said of him. His teachers at school, his parents, everyone. But of course, they really knew nothing...nothing of the amazing future this strange boy would have...nothing of the greatness within him.

And neither did Peter.

"That Peter Huddleston, peculiar isn't he?" said the Huddleston's nosy neighbors, the Crewpots. Mr. and Mrs. Crewpot had a perfectly neat house right next to the Huddlestons. They had a perfectly trimmed lawn with metal gnome ornaments on the unnaturally even grass, which Mrs. Crewpot thought was terribly smart. The house was painted a sickly yellow-brown color that matched the Crewpot's mini-van and their very fat, round cat, Pukey.

The Huddlestons, on the other hand, lived in a two story beige house, with beige carpeting and beige furniture. Gertrude Huddleston, Peter's stepmother, was a tall, stern, white-haired woman, who loved to cook, was peculiarly neat and was very organized. She however, did not seem to pay much attention, if any at all, to Peter. Mr. Huddleston, Peter's father, was a very grave man with faded brown hair who used to be a brilliant businessman, though Peter had no memories of ever seeing him work. He just sat on his tattered brown armchair, the only piece of furniture in the house that wasn't beige, and read the daily newspaper.

Peter was a thin boy of twelve, with shaggy brown hair and light blue eyes. He had a quiet nature and didn't really stand out in anything in particular. He did well at his studies, but most of the time preferred to be alone. Most days, after a wearying set of classes, Peter ran home and went straight up to his room, thankfully closing the door behind him with a tremendous feeling of relief. His small room was filled with comic books and mystery novels, a little bed in the corner and a bed-side table with a beige lamp on it. He liked this side table since it had a hidden drawer facing his bed. It was where he kept his chocolate bars, Swiss army knife, boomerang and a small, framed photograph. The photograph was of Mr. Huddleston and his real mother both pointing to a carving on a large oak tree. The carving was of the letters 'A.H.' and 'P.W.' enclosed in a heart. Peter's mother's maiden name was Patricia Willowbrook, and this was his favorite picture of his parents. His dad was much younger with bushy brown hair, more like Peter's than the dull faded color it was now. Peter's mother was pointing to the tree carving and laughing, as his dad embraced her in a one armed hug. His mom was very pretty; she had brown hair the color of caramel and light blue eyes. Peter never really knew her since she had died when he was very young. He remembered random glimpses of her, smiling and danc-ing, but nothing more. Whenever he looked at this photograph though, he always saw his parents happy and together, and that made him feel stronger.

One day, Peter hurriedly ran home, up the beige steps and into his small room. As he threw off the brown leather book bag that was strapped across his chest, he jumped on his bed, opened his secret bedside drawer, and pulled out a particularly large, thick chocolate bar wrapped in gold foil. He had just finished his last day of school. All the facts, dates and numbers he had forced into his head for his final exams seemed to melt away as he took a big bite from his cream filled treat. "Summer," he murmured, "At last."

He grabbed a comic book from a large, teetering stack on the floor and started to read. Hours passed before he happily took one last bite of chocolate, as his heavy eyelids wandered towards the growing darkness outside his window. Stretching out his arms, he saw the first stars starting to appear in the empty sky. Feeling very tranquil and full of chocolate, Peter effortlessly drifted off to sleep, pulling his soft blanket over his school clothes, as great waves of relief spread over his weary limbs.

It was very early the next morning when Peter woke up. The sky outside was only starting to turn a dark shade of blue, and he could still make out the lingering remains of a few fading stars. As he lazily stretched out, he began to hear the cheery chirping of the birds outside.

"What to do today?" he thought. He slowly rose from his toasty bed, still wearing his school clothes, and went to brush his teeth. As he stumbled out of his warm room into the chilly, beige hall, he peered through the banister to see his father asleep on the armchair in the living room below, as was usual.

"Morning Dad," he said to himself, as he entered the dull hall bathroom that was saturated with flowery air freshener. His stepmother loved spraying thick fogs of flowery air freshener almost as much as she loved the color beige. Peter picked up his toothbrush and started brushing his teeth. Staring into the mirror, he noticed there was chocolate smudged all over his mouth.

Not bothering to change, he quietly crept down the carpeted stairs and into the sterilized kitchen, careful not to wake his father. He opened the sparkling clean refrigerator and came face to face with over a dozen neatly stacked and labeled plastic containers, all containing various dishes of his stepmother's cooking. He disappointedly closed the refrigerator door and decided to just fix himself a cheese sandwich with a glass of milk. It wasn't that Gertrude's cooking was exactly horrible; it was just that everything she made, no matter what it was, always tasted the same. In fact, her cooking had no taste at all. It was always very bland, and served with thick tasteless gravy. "Ugh," he shuddered at the thought, frozen, bland, beige gravy.

The Huddlestons, despite the overabundance of Gertrude's cooking, never really ate together, and Peter was used to eating all of his meals in this fashion. After a few more cheese sandwiches and a couple glasses of milk, he went back upstairs and got his boomerang and Swiss army knife from his bedside table. Clumsily pulling on his black rubber shoes, he tiptoed down the stairs and went quietly out the front door.

Peter felt the cool morning air on his face as he made his way to the nearby lake a few blocks from his home. As he walked, his boomerang jutting out of his pants pocket, the sun was already starting to shine and the trees were completely immersed with the sounds of chirping birds. The Crewpot's house was still quiet except for the meowing of their fat, yellow-brown cat, Pukey, who was staring suspiciously at Peter from their windowsill. All in all, it was a cozy neighborhood and Peter was comfortable here, although he never really felt that he fit in very well. A place he did love was a little sweetshop called 'Creamers,' which was very near the lake. It was a cozy shop full of old wooden tables and brass furnishings, and was always overflowing with delicious sweets. Mr. and Mrs. Twickeypoo, a kindly, though very elderly couple who never heard what their customers were saying, ran Creamers. Even though they were still closed, Peter could see all the magnificent sweets and pastries through the pane glass window. Strolling along, curiously peering into the other boutiques, he passed the beige furniture shop, 'Blandys,' his stepmother's favorite store. Everything in Blandys was very beige and incredibly boring.

As he was just about to turn the corner towards the lake, he was startled.

"Oy! Huddleston!"

It was Mr. Twickeypoo, wearing his silver spectacles and a cream-colored apron over his clothes.

"Morning Mr. Twickeypoo." said Peter, as he turned and walked back towards him.

"What're you doing up so early...umm..."

"Peter?"

"What?"

"Peter."

"Peter what?"

"Me," he said, breaking out in a broad smile.

"I know that! Why?"

"Why what?" laughed Peter.

"Huh?"

"Honestly Henry!" came Mrs. Twickeypoos voice from inside.

Mrs. Twickeypoo was a sweet, chubby lady who was always busy behind the Creamers counter fixing up treats and tidying up the shop. Whenever he came to visit, she always gave him samples of their latest sweets.

"We have a new shipment in this morning, dear, white chocolate shells filled with raspberry, won't you try some?"

Peter gratefully took a shell from the gleaming silver platter.

"Umm..." he managed, through a mouthful of white chocolate. "This is the best one yet!"

"Do get some more then, dear."

"Okay," he replied, happily taking a few more shells.

"You know what?" said Mrs. Twickeypoo, reaching under the counter, "I'll just put some in a bag for you."

"Oh no, that's okay," said Peter, as Mrs. Twickeypoo started shoveling chocolate shells into a small Creamers bag. It was already starting to look over packed.

"My pleasure," she said sweetly, continuing to cram in more chocolates. "You're so thin dear, are you fed well at home? I haven't seen your father in ages, but when I do I'll...HENRY! WHAT DO YOU THINK YOU'RE DOING?"

Peter turned to see Mr. Twickeypoo about to bite into a huge slice of thick chocolate cake.

"You know Dr. Winkles said you have to cut down your sugar levels!" she said exasperatedly.

"But it's been so long!" he cried.

"You just had peach ice cream for breakfast! Remind me to let you try that, Peter dear, I made it myself," she added, pausing momentarily. "Henry, put that cake down!"

"LEAVE ME BE WOMAN!" he shouted back, in a fleeting fit of courage.

"WHAT DID YOU SAY?" she growled, daggers shooting from her eyes.

"Nothing dear." he mumbled, reluctantly putting the slice of chocolate cake down on the small polished wooden table in front of him. As if to protest, he slowly began to unroll the morning paper that was stuffed in his pocket.

"Here you are," Mrs. Twickeypoo continued, handing Peter the bag of chocolate shells that was now full to bursting. "I'll go get you some of that ice cream. Go right ahead and have a seat next to Mr. Twickeypoo and I'll..."

Mrs. Twickeypoo shot a look to her husband, who was completely hidden behind the newspaper he was holding.

"Your paper's upside down, Henry." she said sternly, purposefully marching over to him and taking away the half eaten chocolate cake from behind his newspaper.

"Oh, so it is." he replied, sounding genuinely puzzled.

As Mrs. Twickeypoo hurried off to the ice box, angrily muttering to the plate of half eaten chocolate cake she was holding, Peter took a seat next to his old friend.

"Here you go, sir," he whispered, carefully handing Mr. Twickeypoo a huge handful of chocolate shells from his bag. Mr. Twickeypoo gratefully stuffed a few into his mouth before stashing the rest of them in his apron pocket.

Keeping his voice in a conspiratorial whisper, he said "Thanks. Mrs. Twickeypoo doesn't even let me go behind the counter anymore. Says I eat too many of the pastries."

"WHAT WAS THAT?"

"Nothing dear." he gently answered, sneaking three more chocolate shells.

After much chatter and two enormous bowls of homemade peach ice cream, Peter said his goodbyes to the Twickeypoos and thanked them again for the abundant sweets. They continued waving at him from their shop door until he turned the corner at Blandys. Holding his re-stuffed bag of chocolate shells, and feeling very content, he made his way towards the lake.

The lake looked completely serene as Peter approached its smooth, reflective edge. A slight breeze passed, as he realized he was the only one there. He preferred it like this. By himself, exploring. It was certainly what he had grown accustomed to. He felt strangely at peace in these moments. He didn't feel the need to put up a protective wall. Peter took a slow, deep breath and let it out with a heavy sigh as he pulled the boomerang out from his pants pocket. He loved this boomerang and took it with him everywhere. Mr. Twickeypoo had given it to him years ago, and he had practiced using it everyday since. It was a handsomely made object, and quite elegant, as far as boomerangs go. It was carved from hardened oak, yet was very light. Its edges were lined in gold paint, and on its face was an eagle that looked like it was just about to spread its wings and take flight. Aside from the photograph of his parents in his secret drawer, this was his most prized possession. He had also grown very adept at using it.

Peter filled his lungs with another deep breath before leaning back and throwing his boomerang straight over the lake. With a whooshing hallow sound, it spun in a tight spiral climbing effortlessly high into the air. As it arced high over the lake it turned, and just as rapidly zoomed back, landing softly in his hand.

Comforted by the natural way the boomerang felt in his hand, Peter spotted a plump red apple growing at the center of a leafy tree on his side of the lake, the apple stood out like a beacon from the other apples which were not yet ripe.

"Red apple." he murmured, taking just a moment to aim. The boomerang launched towards the bushy tree and was securely back in his hand before the bright red fruit plopped gently on a pile of leaves below it.

Peter spent the rest of the morning amusing himself in this manner, as he had so many other mornings, until his arm began to ache and groups of people started to arrive to spend the day by the lake. Having already inhaled half of his chocolate shells yet growing increasingly hungry, he tucked away his boomerang and headed home. Just as he was turning the corner at Blandys, he heard a severe laugh echoing from inside the overpriced store.

"Oh no. Aunt Celeste." he thought.

Aunt Celeste owned Blandys and, in truth, was not really Peter's aunt. She was his stepmother's best friend and the two of them were always together. She was a tall woman with puffed up, flaming red hair, and she always wore huge round sunglasses. Overly melodramatic and forever draped in flowing silk scarves, she was also possessed of erratic moods. Gathering speed, putting his head down and turning his face completely away, he almost made it past the obnoxious store window, when...

"Peter darling! Is that you?" Aunt Celeste cried, in a shrill, fake voice.

"You know perfectly well it's me," he thought.

Aunt Celeste had risen from her beige desk and was gliding swiftly towards him. She was wearing a glaring, green suit, with a huge, bright orange scarf wrapped around her neck. The scarf clashed horribly with her hair; the sight of her was truly blinding.

"Hi Aunt Celeste." he said drearily, his lips barely moving.

"Peter! I knew it was you! How's your father?"

"Oh he's..."

"Oh good, I just spoke to your mother on the phone..."

"Stepmother."

"Whatever dear. Gertrude said she'd be coming down this afternoon. I want to show her these wonderful footstools that have just arrived," she continued, dramatically waving her hand in the direction of some beige footstools exactly like the ones in Peter's house.

"I think we already have those," he said casually.

"Oh no, no, no dearie," she squealed, throwing her hair back and laughing harshly. Aunt Celeste laughed like old smoking men coughed.

"You have the beige footstools."

"Those are beige," he said, in a matter of fact voice. "Everything here is beige."

"Those are not beige," she replied, the airiness dropping from her voice, as his statement was the ultimate offense in her ethereal world.

"Yes they are."

"One footstool is faded salmon!" she retorted indignantly. "And the other is faded peach!"

"Its beige!" he said impatiently, "Beige, beige, beige everything, all of it, my whole house! There's no such color as faded salmon!"

"Yes there is!" she stammered indignantly.

"Yeah, it's called BEIGE!"

"WELL!" she spat huffily. "If it wasn't for my furniture and Gertrude's good taste, your whole house would look like that ratty armchair your father hangs onto. It's like a brown pimple on a perfect peach"

"My mother gave him that chair," said Peter through tightly clenched teeth.

"Well, that explains it."

"Explains what?" fumed Peter, turning just as red as Aunt Celeste's hair.

"Her taste was always dodgy, look who she married! I always tell Gertrude... Of course, not to put down your father dear, but..."

"You take that back!"

"Take what back, dearie?" she asked slyly, her over lipsticked mouth breaking out in a cruel smirk. "I'm just telling you what is glaringly apparent. At least to anyone with real beauty, brains and breed... AHHHHHHHHH!"

Before Peter could stop himself, his boomerang popped into his hand and he threw it at Aunt Celeste's frilly desk. The spinning wing scythed forward, narrowly missing her head and cleanly beheading an entire vase of dull, lifeless flowers. His boomerang was back in his hand before the faded bulbs even reached the floor. Too late, Aunt Celeste started shrieking hysterically, diving hair first behind a high beige couch.

"Don't ever talk about my parents like that again!" Peter said fiercely, storming out of the shop. He could still hear her high-pitched screeching as he approached Creamers and saw Mr. and Mrs. Twickeypoo standing inquisitively by their shop door.

"What's all the racket about, dear?" asked Mrs. Twickeypoo in a concerned voice.

"What racket? Quiet as a tomb out here." said a befuddled
Mr. Twickeypoo, amid bouts of Aunt Celeste's escalating screaming.

"She insulted my parents, so...so, I threw my boomerang at her
flowers."

"Oh dear," said Mrs. Twickeypoo, looking even more concerned.

"Serves her right," said Mr. Twickeypoo resolutely. "If I had a boomerang, I'd aim it straight for that red hair of hers and..."

"Henry!" barked Mrs. Twickeypoo. In almost the same breath, "Are
you alright dear?" she asked soothingly. "Would you like to talk about it
over some cake?"

"No thanks," said Peter, wanting to be alone, "I think I'd best be getting home. Um...thanks again for the chocolates." he said apologetically,
holding up the little Creamers bag.

"Our pleasure," she gently replied.

"Come back soon, you hear?" added Mr. Twickeypoo. "And don't you
worry, Mrs. Twickeypoo and I are on your side. Whatever that woman
said...well...don't give it a second thought. She's just a bitter woman, and
yesterday I overcharged her...a lot."

"Henry!"

Despite himself, Peter couldn't help smiling. "Thanks." he said.

"Of course." said Mr. Twickeypoo, with a wink. "A lot!"

Peter made his way home as the Twickeypoos silently watched him
from their shop door.

He could not believe what Aunt Celeste had said about his parents.
She had no right, he thought. Walking angrily back to his house, he
decided he'd spend the rest of the day reading comic books in his room.
Just then, something landed heavily on the sidewalk in front of him and
rolled towards his feet.

"Hey Huddleston, pass it back would you?" yelled a blond-haired
boy from the middle of a grassy field. About half a dozen kids were playing catch and Peter recognized most of them from his school, though
he couldn't recall their names. He was quite surprised that the blond-
haired boy knew his name, well, his last name anyway. He bent down,
picked the dusty softball off the sidewalk and whipped it to the boy
who had called out to him, the ball splatted into the boy's glove with

impressive force. As Peter started to walk away, the same boy called out to him again.

"Hey Huddleston...Peter, isn't it?"

"Um...Yeah,"

"You wanna play some ball with us?"

"Can't, have to be getting back." he said automatically, pointing in the direction of his house.

"Alright." his classmate replied, shrugging his shoulders.

Peter watched them play for a few more seconds, just carelessly tossing the softball back and forth, before starting toward his house again. This was how it was nowadays, he just preferred being on his own. It's not that he didn't like the boys at school; he thought they were alright. It's just that he never really considered making friends with them. He didn't think he was upsetting anyone, as he couldn't imagine why anyone would care whether or not they were friends of his at all. He was startled that the blond-haired boy knew his full name. All throughout the school year he would hear, "C'mon Huddleston, have some pizza with us," or "Peter, we're all going down to the theater to watch a movie, wanna come?" But Peter never did have pizza or watch movies with his classmates from school. He just never felt like it. It wasn't that he didn't love pizzas or movies, he did, quite a lot; he just enjoyed them on his own. It wasn't always like this though. He remembered moments of reading together with his dad, or playing outside with his mother. Though they were such hazy memories they felt more like wistful dreams. A story remembered rather than an actual part of his life. And yet, things now weren't so gruesomely bad. He attended school regularly and got good marks in his classes. He also got to visit the Twickeypoos often. It was just different, that's all. Nothing to go on about, he thought, just different.

A few blocks from his house, Peter stopped to climb a tree he occasionally liked to sit in. It was a tall, narrow tree, with an abundance of sturdy branches near its top. Its leaves were bushy and wide, and when Peter sat on the top branch, they hid him entirely. Settling himself, he surveyed the view from this hidden spot. He could make out the shimmer of the lake in the distance, and the top of Blandys. "Stupid woman," he thought. He saw Creamers. He saw the patch of grass where the boys were playing ball, and near it, his school. Turning around, he saw his house, quiet and still, and the Crewpot's yellowy-brown home, and all their little metal gnomes scattered around the front lawn.

"My world," he whispered to himself.

About an hour later Peter quietly closed the front door behind him. Stealthily he peeked into the living room, but his dad's brown armchair was empty. Walking up to it, he reached into his Creamers bag and pulled out the plump red apple. Cleaning it on his shirt, he placed it carefully on the soft, thick armrest, and smiled.

"Peter!"

Whipping around he saw his father standing stiffly and looking very upset.

"Y-yeah Dad,"

"Did you attack Aunt Celeste?"

"What! No!" he said defensively.

"She called here, hysterical, screaming that you charged into Blandys and tried to take her head off with that, that..."

"Boomerang." he said dryly.

"So you did do it."

"I did not!" said Peter. "I threw it at the flowers on her desk."

"Why?"

For a moment, he didn't answer and looked down at the beige rug on the floor. He wasn't sure if he wanted his dad to know why Aunt Celeste had upset him.

"She talked badly about you and mom," he said, kicking idly at a bump in the rug. Peter couldn't even remember the last time they had spoken about his mother. He looked up and saw his father staring at him.

"Go to your room," his father said with no emotion in his voice.

"What!" said Peter, thinking this was completely unfair. He was going to go to his room anyway, but that wasn't the point.

"Gertrude is very upset. Celeste is telling anyone who'll listen that you attacked her."

"If I had wanted to hit her on the head, I wouldn't have missed," Peter mumbled.

His father looked at him, all expression drifting off his face. He moved to sit down on his armchair, knocking over the shiny red apple Peter had left for him, not even noticing it.

"I'm very disappointed in you, Peter."

Peter felt the blood rush to his face. All he could do was stare at the apple on the floor next to his dad's chair. He wanted to shake him. He wanted to shout at him as hard as he could. But he didn't. All he could do was stare at the apple on the floor, a bruise already forming on its flawless surface.

"Well you shouldn't be," said Peter confidently. His father looked up at him, the expression on his face had changed; yet he said nothing.

Peter turned around and walked out of the living room. Gertrude was standing at the foot of the stairs in a beige apron; her face was stern, as if expecting some sort of an apology.

"Heard everything?" he spat sarcastically. "Or did we not speak loudly enough for you?"

And with that, Peter walked up to his room without waiting for Gertrude's reaction. He put his chocolate shells, Swiss army knife and boomerang back into his secret drawer and closed it quickly, ignoring the old photograph of his parents. As he sat on his bed, looking out his window, his mind went blank. It wasn't until a noise from a passing car woke him from his daze that he realized it was nighttime.

2

UNEXPECTED NEWS

The next day, Peter woke up in bed unable to remember falling asleep. A bright sun was encouraging the birds' chirping as he hastily changed his clothes, grabbed his boomerang, Swiss knife and chocolate shells, and headed down the stairs. He was going to have a quick breakfast, but Gertrude was in the kitchen talking importantly on the phone. The handset was clutched tightly in her hand, her white hair was pulled severely in a bun, and she slowly stuffed dry, stale looking crackers into her mouth, without effecting the speed at which she was talking into the phone. Peter caught words like...

"...it would be better, but..." and "...I don't really know her, she's always been so strange, but then look at her nephew..."

Just then, Gertrude turned and saw Peter standing next to the front door, listening. She stopped in mid-sentence and looked at him like she was about to tell him something, but stuffed another stale cracker into her mouth, and, lowering her voice, resumed her whispered conversation on the phone.

Having already seen each other, Peter walked to the refrigerator, found some cheese, and made himself a couple of his usual cheese sandwiches. He had already stuffed one into his mouth as the front door shut behind him. Wondering what to do today, he figured it wasn't such a good idea to go near Blandys and Aunt Celeste, which meant he couldn't spend the day by the lake or at Creamers. For now though, he decided to walk up to his special tree and climb to one of the top branches. He had just settled onto a particularly sturdy branch when he started wondering what Gertrude was talking about. She usually just pretended he didn't exist, but today she had stopped speaking when she saw him, like he might have overheard something important. What could she have been talking about? After considering the few realistic possibilities, he decided she was probably gossiping with Aunt Celeste, plotting his downfall. Having already finished his sandwiches, he started munching on the rest of his raspberry filled white chocolate shells. The neighborhood was quiet, as usual. Only a few people were walking around, lazily searching for something to do. Peter had just eaten his last chocolate shell when he glanced over at the Crewpot's house and saw a startling sight. Mrs. Crewpot was staring right at him through her second floor window, holding an enormous pair of round, black sunglasses to her face. It wasn't easy to see her, as she was wearing a yellow-brown dress and large straw hat the exact color of her house.

She couldn't possibly see me, Peter thought. Squinting back at her, he saw they weren't sunglasses, but...

"Binoculars!" he muttered. "Great, big binoculars...and she's staring right at me!" Knowing plump, nosy Mrs. Crewpot would never be able to see through the thick, green leaves, even with those massive things, Peter figured she must have seen him climb onto the tree and was straining to see what he was up to. Aunt Celeste probably called her and dramatically reenacted how he had viciously tried to kill her.

"Oh no," he laughed, "Another reason for Mrs. Crewpot to stick her nose into other peoples' business."

Seizing the opportunity that was presenting itself, Peter quickly reached for his boomerang. Moments later it was hurtling its way towards Mrs. Crewpot! Turning back around only about a foot in front of her, it was already halfway back to the tree when she started screaming like a banshee.

"AHHHHHH!!! Harold! Harold!" she screamed, calling for her husband.

Boomerang in hand, Peter was laughing so hard he nearly fell off the branch. He could hear Mrs. Crewpot's screaming escalate as she ran frantically around her house. He even heard Pukey, hissing and spitting at all the commotion she was making. He felt thoroughly proud of himself. Having climbed halfway down the tree, he was still chuckling hysterically, recalling the thunderstruck look on her face. He was about to jump onto the sidewalk when...

"Peter! Get down from there, now!"

Peter turned to see his father standing a few feet away from him, his eyes blazing.

For the next few days, Peter was confined to his room, reading old comic books and throwing his boomerang out the window. His father had grounded him, and Mrs. Crewpot got into the habit of calling their house every couple of hours to remind his father what a terror his son was. By now the whole neighborhood thought Peter was completely mad. Aunt Celeste's stories about their encounter were getting more exaggerated by the minute. A neighbor had told Peter's father how he heard that Peter had repeatedly attacked her with a chainsaw. Mrs. Crewpot's repetitive phone calls to everybody about 'deranged Peter Huddleston' assaulting her from a tree did not help matters any. Peter even caught a few younger children whispering excitedly to one another and pointing up at him through his bedroom window. He, on the other hand, thought this was all thoroughly ridiculous and decided he had had enough.

After nightfall, Peter climbed stealthily down a blue bed sheet he dangled from his window. He was going to confront Aunt Celeste and demand that she take back all the exaggerated lies she had spread about him. He also decided to leave his boomerang in his room, knowing the very sight of it would send her into a state of absolute hysteria. Running over to the next street past his house, he thought it best to avoid the Crewpots, knowing Mrs. Crewpot was sure to be dedicatedly patrolling the streets with her binoculars. It was a cool, breezy night without a star in the sky. Trying to avoid everyone who now considered him dangerous, he turned his head away from the few people who were lazily shuffling down the sidewalks.

He checked his watch and saw that the lakeside shops would be closing in about ten minutes. Quickening his pace, he noticed that this side of the block was undergoing street repairs and yellow plastic safety ribbons had been put up everywhere. Not wanting to fall into an open pothole in the growing darkness, he was forced to run around all the numerous safety clearings spread out in front of him. Stumbling and out of breath, he turned the street corner and caught sight of the lakeside shops. Creamers, as well as some of the other boutiques, were already closed. Squinting, Peter could just make out that Blandys was still open. Two people were getting ready to leave the shop, both carrying beige vases in their arms. A red haired woman had just stepped out the door. It was unmistakably Aunt Celeste. This was his chance.

He had just started walking resolutely toward her when-WHAM! He slipped and pitched face first into wet cement. Sprawled on the newly paved sidewalk, Peter felt something tangled all over him. Yellow safety ribbon and cement were wrapped around his legs, sticking to his pants. "No!" he cried. As he pulled at the sticky ribbons, it felt like he was making it worse and knotting it all around him. Glancing around, he saw the two figures turning their backs, about to leave. Pulling his Swiss army knife out from his pocket, he fumbled with its little grooves until he managed to pull out the small metal blade. Quickly cutting through the knotted ribbon, he sprang up and sprinted towards Blandys. Halfway there, huffing and puffing, Peter tried to get Aunt Celeste's attention before she walked away.

"Celeste! I want to talk to you!" he yelled.

It happened in a matter of seconds.

Aunt Celeste had turned around, taken one look at Peter and let out a bloodcurdling scream. The large vase she was holding came crashing to the ground, sending beige shards flying everywhere. He heard hushed cries all around him from the few people still closing up the remaining stores.

"Peter! What are you doing?"

Peter looked up to see who had said this and his jaw hit the floor. It was Gertrude. She was still holding on to a vase and had a look of absolute astonishment on her face. Then, horribly, Peter realized he was still holding his knife.

✳ ✳ ✳

"CAKED IN CEMENT, IN THE MIDDLE OF THE NIGHT, SHREDDED SAFTEY RIBBON TANGLED ALL AROUND YOUR CLOTHES, HOLDING A KNIFE AND RUNNING TOWARDS AUNT CELESTE SCREAMING AT HER! PETER! HAVE YOU LOST YOUR MIND COMPLETELY?"

Peter had never seen his father this shocked and angry before. Sitting uncomfortably on a hard cushioned chair in their living room, he watched as his father continued pacing back and forth, ranting at him. Gertrude, standing nearby, looked on in a perpetual state of disbelief.

"What were you thinking?" he roared.

"I just wanted to talk to her about..."

"Talk to her!" he yelled, "She has over a dozen witnesses saying they saw you trying to attack her with a knife! Do you know what they're saying? They're saying that that lunatic Huddleston boy has completely lost his senses, turned savage and assaulted his own aunt and stepmother!"

"She's not really my aunt..."

"THAT'S NOT THE POINT! Gertrude had to plead with Celeste not to press charges! As it is, she's thinking about filing a restraining order with the police! The entire town thinks you're crazy!"

Peter thought this was totally unfair, not to mention taken completely out of context. After all, he only wanted to talk to Aunt Celeste, and the 'weapon' in question was a small blade from a Swiss army knife.

"You scared Gertrude and me to death! I walked into your room to find you missing, and a sheet was hanging out of your window! You were grounded! Then I received a frantic phone call from Gertrude telling me about what had happened! I thought I was going crazy! No, no, no Peter, this is too much! I don't know what's gotten into you lately! First Celeste, then Mrs. Crewpot...I saw you throw your boomerang from that tree myself..."

"It would've never hit her..."

"How does she know that? She's telling the whole neighborhood you tried to hurt her! And now this! What am I going to do with you? I'm starting to think Hillside isn't such a bad idea after all!"

"What? What's Hillside..."

"Go to your room!"

"But what's..."

"Your room-NOW!"

Peter couldn't sleep a wink. He lay on his bed in the dark, staring at the light creeping under his door from the hall. He could hear the muffled sounds of his father speaking with Gertrude and making numerous phone calls late into the night. Peter anxiously wondered what on Earth 'Hillside' could be. He thought it must be some sort of boarding school or military academy. He was terrified; he didn't want to leave for some strange, new school. Mean teachers, no Creamers, they definitely would not allow his boomerang. He'd probably never see the Twickeypoos again! This was not fair! His thoughts were racing back and forth in his head, until, exhausted and weary, he finally began to fall asleep. His eyes closing...closing...

All of a sudden, he was marching with a troop of soldiers all wearing stiff beige uniforms. He tried to see who they were, but to his horror, none of them had faces, only blank gray masks and empty holes where their eyes should have been.

"You have your test today, Huddleston!" came a cold, ominous voice.

"What? No one told me! What test? I didn't know!" Peter cried.

"Welcome to Hillside, boy. You'll be staying here...permanently!"

Suddenly, Peter realized he was sinking. The dark ground was sucking him in like quicksand, as his own troop viciously taunted him, pointing and jeering, silent laughter rising from their blank faces. Instinctively, he reached for his boomerang and threw it as hard as he could toward the ominous voice and waited for its return. He watched as it grew smaller and smaller in the growing distance. But it never came back.

"Noooooo!!!" he yelled, as he sank further and further into the ground.

"NOOOOOOO!!!"

Peter sat bolt upright. It was morning. The bright light of the new day was filling his cluttered room. It was just a dream. As he shakily wiped the sweat from his forehead, he turned away from his window and gasped. His father was sitting on the end of his bed, his back facing him. As he spoke, his voice sounded troubled.

"Peter...we have to talk."

"About what?" he asked defensively.

"I don't know what's gotten into you lately. It's not just what happened with Aunt Celeste or Mrs. Crewpot, although I'm not happy with that either. It's that you're always by yourself, on your own."

"That's not true. Besides, with all the exaggerated stories Aunt Celeste and Mrs. Crewpot are telling everyone, it's a wonder a mob isn't after me."

"I know...but you have to admit, it does look suspicious..."

"That doesn't mean it's true!"

"Even Gertrude is shocked by what she saw."

"When isn't she?"

His father took a deep breath.

"I think it would be best for everyone if you went away for the summer."

Peter's heart started to pound in his chest. He could feel the blood rushing to his face. He was going to be punished his entire summer vacation because he stood up for his parents.

"It's a place called..."

"Hillside, I know." he interrupted, restraining an urge to start yelling.

"Hillside Manor, how did you..."

"I don't care what it is, I'm not going!"

"You don't..."

"No!" Peter yelled, turning red in the face. "All I do is spend the year going to that boring school, my grades are pretty good too! And everyday I come home and no one says a word to me..."

"That's not..."

"YOU LET ME FINISH!"

His father was shocked. Peter had never raised his voice to him before.

"Of course I'm on my own all the time, it's not like you take any interest in me! And Gertrude! She pretends I'm not even here!"

Peter was worked up; he had thrown off his bed sheets and was standing up, yelling at his father and getting more red in the face by the second.

"And now Celeste! Who Gertrude insists I call 'aunt', starts telling everyone I'm crazy just because I stood up to her for putting down you and mom! So fine, you want to send me away to some stupid correctional military summer school? Fine! I wouldn't want to embarrass you here even more anyway!"

Peter was breathing so hard he could hardly get the words out. His father was still wearing the same grave expression, except now his eyes had started to water and his face was tense.

"Peter," he started, after having to clear his throat, "I...I never meant..." He couldn't find the words he needed.

Peter stood there in his mismatched pajamas, staring at the crumpled man sitting on the end of his bed. He did not like seeing his father like this.

"Dad, I..."

"Hillside Manor isn't a correctional facility or a military school, it's an actual manor. It belongs to your aunt, your real aunt."

Peter couldn't believe what he was hearing. "My aunt?" he said slowly, "I have a real aunt? From your family?"

A long silence washed over the room.

"No."

Peter's mouth was hanging wide open. He was flooded with so many thoughts, he was sure it was affecting his hearing.

"But that means, she's, she'd be..."

"Your mother's sister."

In that moment, Peter's mind went blank. He stood there transfixed, staring at his father. All the blood was draining from his face. He needed to steady himself on his bedside table to keep from falling over.

"Why don't you sit down?" his father offered, gesturing towards the bed. He did so automatically. Sometime passed, as Peter began to tightly hug his pillow, still staring open mouthed at his father.

"Peter?"

"Uh-huh,"

"Are you alright?"

"Uh-huh,"

"Are you sure?"

"Uh-huh,"

"You want a glass of wa..."

"Why didn't you tell me?" he asked, limply.

"The truth is, she asked us not to."

"Why?"

"Your Aunt Gillian is, that's her name, Gillian Willowbrook...she's...a bit unusual. Her life is quite different from ours and...we don't see eye to eye a lot. When your mother passed away, we had words with each other and decided it would be better this way."

"But why?"

"She's very different, she has strange... she doesn't get along well with Gertrude."

"So what about Gertrude!" Peter said sternly, "How could you not tell me mom had a sister!"

"Gillian and your mother hadn't seen each other for a long time. They hardly spoke at all, actually. Your mother thought it would be better if we didn't mention her to you. When you were born, your mother and I hadn't seen her in quite some time."

"Is she nuts?" Peter asked.

"What? No...I don't think...no, of course not."

"Well, why should I meet her now?"

"Look..." said his father, suddenly seeming very tired. The effort of having to think about these memories drained him immensely. "You're spending the summer with your aunt and that's that."

"But..."

"No 'buts' Peter. She's the only relative we have. You need to go somewhere, get away from the mess here. Gillian will be able to watch you better, keep you out of trouble."

"But I don't..."

"You're going. You've gotten into enough trouble here to last a lifetime. I never thought you'd meet her, but seeing the way things are developing...I'm worried about you, and so is Gertrude."

"Gertrude! Worried about me? HA!"

"You're not taking your mothers...you don't seem to be handling things well. Obviously you don't care for Gertrude. I never see you with any friends your own age. It would be better if you met your aunt. It might...we hope it might help you."

"I don't need..."

"Peter, it's done. The arrangements have been made. You're going. I mean it."

And with that, his father left the room. As the door shut behind him, Peter was left dazed and confused, sitting on the side of his bed.

For the next few days, Peter tried wrapping his mind around what had happened. He was a quiet, fairly good student, who minded his own business and had just started his summer vacation. Less than a week later, he was the town lunatic who attacked his aunt with a knife, or chainsaw, whichever version of the story you happened to hear, violently assaulted his neighbor, and was being carted off to the boondocks to his long lost, mad aunt, who he just found out existed.

Peter desperately tried reasoning with his father, but he wouldn't hear of it and made clear that the subject was closed for discussion. Peter didn't like this one bit. He hated the idea of running away just because of the stories that were going around. But at the same time... he had an aunt, a real live aunt. He never had one before. His father was an only child and he thought his mother was too. Endless questions filled his mind. Why hadn't his mother and aunt spoken for so long? Why didn't they keep in touch with each other? And why had Aunt Gillian asked his father not to even mention her to her own nephew? A flood of possibilities invaded his thoughts, but everything kept leading back to one explanation...she must be completely bonkers...stark raving mad. What was his summer going to be like? Stuck in a decrepit old house, probably condemned, being chased around by his crazy, old aunt, her blue hair in curlers, fanatically wielding an ancient wooden roller. Hundreds of her vicious cats, her 'babies', clawing at him as he lay huddled in a dusty bed with moldy sheets. He would probably have to floss years of dried, chewed up prunes from her crusty dentures. He shuddered at the thought.

Not even a telephone call with the Twickeypoos could tear his mind from these archaic images. By now, the Twickeypoos had heard numerous versions of the stories circulating about Peter, and thought they were all completely ridiculous. Mrs. Twickeypoo was just as startled as he was when he called her at home and told her about his newfound aunt.

"...so now I have to live with my Aunt Gillian for the summer. I don't want to. I mean, I really want to meet my mom's sister, but, well, she sounds a bit...um...off. Hello? Mrs. Twickeypoo?"

"Yes dear, I'm here."

"What do you think, Mrs. Twickeypoo?"

"Well, it seems...honestly I'm not sure."

"Peter!"

His father had walked into the kitchen and was eying him talking on the phone.

"No phone privileges, you're still grounded!"

"Sorry Mrs. Twickeypoo, I have to go now. Say 'hi' to Mr. Twickeypoo for me."

"Yes, of course, dear."

Three days later, Peter was packed. He would be leaving early the following morning. He had stuffed his clothes and some comic books into a bulging suitcase and had emptied the contents of his secret drawer into his cleaned out, brown leather book bag. In it were some Creamers chocolate bars, his Swiss army knife and his parents photograph. His boomerang was jutting out of his pants pocket, as was usual.

He had just managed to force his suitcase shut when he heard the doorbell ring. Poking his head out from his bedroom, he saw his father heading for the front door.

"Peter, the Twackeyloos are here to see you."

"That's Twickeypoo, dear," said Mrs. Twickeypoo.

Racing down the stairs, Peter ran in front of his father and pulled open the front door to reveal Mr. and Mrs. Twickeypoo smiling brightly at him. He was so excited; the Twickeypoos had never come to his house before. He hugged both of them as his father hovered behind him, still failing to invite the elderly couple inside.

"We just wanted to wish you well before you left, dear." said Mrs. Twickeypoo, nervously glancing away from Peter's scowling father. "Now you be careful and give us a call whenever you like. We also wanted to give you a little something for the trip. Henry...Henry!"

"What!"

"Give Peter his gift."

Mr. Twickeypoo handed him a medium sized paper bag he was holding. Peter reached in and pulled out what looked like a very nice music box. It was about two inches high and made of polished wood.

"Oh wow!"

"Open it, son," said Mr. Twickeypoo, beaming.

Peter opened the polished wooden lid, which was hinged to one side of the box, and almost gasped. In it, the box was sectioned off into twelve separate squares and lined in red velvet, each square sheltering a single chocolate. But not just any chocolates, a dozen of the most magnificent chocolates he had ever seen. Each one was beautifully decorated, bearing different colors and designs.

"Thank you!" he exclaimed. "They're amazing!"

"Now, dear," said Mrs. Twickeypoo, "These are just for you, they're very special chocolates."

"I can see that!"

"It would break my heart if you ate them up all at once, just save them for very special occasions. They'll taste better if you eat them one at a time. You know...they don't mix well together."

"Okay." said Peter, gawking at his fantastic present.

"Best if you just keep them close until you need them."

Peter, grinning, noticed Mr. Twickeypoo give him a wink.

Mrs. Twickeypoo glanced up at Peter's father. A moment of awkward silence passed between them.

"Alright then, take care dear, have a good summer and we'll see you when you get back."

"Good day, sir." Mr. Twickeypoo added politely to Peter's father.

Peter was still waving to the Twickeypoos as they walked down the street. As his father locked the front door, he ran excitedly up to his room, jumped on his bed, and stared in awe at his new gift. Each of the twelve chocolates was completely different. One was the shape of a leaf, green and plump, the other was the shape of a clover. Another looked like a marshmallow. All except for one looked inviting. It was in the middle of the box, round and black with a skull and crossbones on it. He thought Mr. Twickeypoo must have decorated this one; it was probably really bitter dark chocolate. After admiring them all for some time, he shut the polished wooden box with a snap, and put it in his brown leather book bag with the rest of his things.

The next morning, Peter woke with a start. The sun was just coming up and his father was already dressed. Peter had barely slept a wink. Trudging his suitcase down to their beige car, his leather book bag slung across his chest, he tried to prepare himself for whatever lay ahead. They would be traveling to Hillside Manor entirely by car. His father told him it would be a three-day trip. He could not remember the two of them ever having to spend so much time together, and found himself feeling slightly nervous.

"Say goodbye to Gertrude, Peter."

"Goodbye Gertrude," he said, exasperatedly.

"Goodbye," she replied, without looking at him.

A few moments later and they were off. Peter buckled into the passenger seat next to his somber father. As they drove by the lakeside shops, he glanced longingly at Creamers, failing to notice the two looming figures staring at him from the darkened store window.

"He's too young, Henry," said Mrs. Twickeypoo gravely. "They'll try to destroy him, I know it."

"Gillian knows what she's doing," said Mr. Twickeypoo confidently. "Besides, there's no other way."

3

HILLSIDE MANOR

The three-day journey to Hillside Manor was anything but fun. Staying at inexpensive bed and breakfast's was all well and good, but even Peter was surprised at how little he and his father had spoken. It was early morning of the third day when his father started to vigorously consult his map.

"We should be arriving soon," he said.

Peter did not like the look of this area at all. The serene greenery of the countryside had melted away hours ago, to reveal what looked like an abandoned town. Decrepit and condemned shacks were littered all along the dusty roadway. Then even the abandoned town disappeared and gradually melted into a rocky, barren desert.

Hour after hour slowly ticked by as they traveled deeper and deeper into a mountainous, rocky wasteland.

"Are you sure we're going the right way?" Peter asked tentatively.

"Yup, these are the only directions Gillian gave me."

Peter reached for the road map and started to unfold it.

"That won't help, this area isn't marked on the map."

A seemingly endless period of time passed before Peter started to make out something in the distance. As hard as he tried, he couldn't be sure of what he saw. As they drove closer, he saw that part of a huge mountain in front of them was chiseled into a towering wall and was covered in thick, green vines. It looked like an enormous barrier that would be used to protect an ancient town.

"Looks like this is it," his father said dryly, trying to hide a spasm of doubt in his voice.

Peter's heart sank. He pictured himself living with his crazy, blue haired aunt, in a small, tattered shack nestled in a condemned town like the one they passed so many hours ago. The Twickeypoos chocolates were probably the only food he'd have all summer. He'd have to catch wild rabbit with his boomerang, and drink stale, brown water from a moldy well. He'd have to...

"Peter...Peter, are you listening to me? Look, this must be the gate."

Peter looked up and saw that they were stopped in front of huge, gray metal gates the exact color as the enormous mountain walls surrounding them. Their sheer size made Peter feel like he was riding a small, beige potato bug. His father pressed down on the horn twice. The sound echoed all around them, but the gates did not open. His father waited a few moments before he honked the horn again. Nothing. Just when Peter started to celebrate that they were in the wrong place, he heard a small, rusty creaking beginning to emanate from in front of them. The metallic groan proceeded to grow louder and louder, until the enormous gray gates slowly and heavily pulled apart.

Peter's jaw dropped. The gates parted to reveal a long driveway, leading up to the entrance of what was by far the biggest building he had ever seen. As their little car pulled up, he noticed the rocky roadway had become paved and smooth. Large, colorful plants and flowers were growing on either side of them, and scattered here and there, life sized marble statues of men and women were all facing the entrance of the manor. The drive to the front door was so long that it took several minutes to reach it. Once his father stopped the car, Peter slowly stepped out and gazed at the mammoth structure. Its sheer magnitude was overwhelming. The property must have been the size of an entire neighborhood. Everywhere he looked he saw twists and turns leading to different paths that ventured deeper into the grounds. The elaborate entrance was an abundance of cream-colored marble steps, leading up to high arched, polished wooden doors. The stories of walls held endless rows of arched windows perched high above the ground. Peter turned and saw his father gawking at the manor, his face stuck in the same awestruck position his was in.

"This can't possibly be the place," said Peter, resolutely.

His father was about to reply, when the high arched, polished wooden doors began to open. A man and woman, both very distinguished looking, emerged from the manor and started to make their way down the marble steps. The man was tall, with neatly parted dark hair that was graying at the sides. He had a perfectly combed mustache and was wearing a starched white shirt, black tie and crisply pressed black suit. The woman, on the other hand, was shorter and rather plump, with silver hair that was tied tightly in two peculiar buns on each side of her head. She was wearing half moon spectacles, and was dressed in a very stiff black blazer and skirt, with an equally crisp white shirt. She was holding a silver clipboard and wore a very serious expression on her face. To Peter's surprise, she went right up to him and addressed him confidently.

"Good afternoon, Master Huddleston." she said politely.

"Uh, hello,"

"Good afternoon, sir." she said, addressing his father.

The mustachioed man watched, smiling, with his hands folded behind his back while the silver-haired woman continued,

"My name is Fredericka Smith, secretary of the house. This is Montgomery Clearwater..." she said, gesturing to the mustachioed man, who at the mention of his name gave both Peter and his father a slight bow, "...who will be acting as your House Host. On behalf of both of us, as well as the entire staff, we welcome you to Hillside Manor."

"Oh, well, thank you very much," said Peter's father, unsure that this was the appropriate response.

"Please follow me," said Mrs. Smith, as she walked back up the cream colored steps. "Mr. Clearwater, if you would," Mr. Clearwater happily went to gather Peter's suitcase from the backseat of the beige car. Peter quickly picked up his leather book bag and flung the strap across his chest.

"Will this be all your luggage, Master Huddleston?" asked Mr. Clearwater jovially.

"Uh, yeah...yes, Mr. Clearwater," said Peter.

"Oh please, sir, do feel free to call me Montgomery or even Monty if you prefer. I would be much obliged. After you, sir," he said cheerfully, gesturing up the steps.

"Thank you Mr. Clear...um, Monty," said Peter, as he and his father followed Mrs. Smith through the high arched doors, with Monty closely behind them.

They entered a huge entrance hall lined with draping of deep blue and gold. Large tapestries were hung all around, featuring various scenes of lovely gardens and deep lakes.

"These are the house tapestries," said Mrs. Smith cordially. "They feature various areas of the manor."

"That one has wild animals all over it," said Peter, pointing out a particularly large tapestry.

"Yes, Master Huddleston," said Mrs. Smith, "This particular tapestry features the most exuberant creatures in our animal preserve."

"Oh," said Peter, not having realized a manor of this size would probably have its own animal preserve.

"Please follow me this way." she continued, "We've prepared an early dinner for you, as you must be quite famished from your travels." Mrs. Smith led them through the entrance hall into another enormously long hall full of the same high arched doors leading off into other stately rooms. Crystal chandeliers lit the hall, and small marble tables were adorned with vase after vase of colorful flowers and glowing candles. Mrs. Smith turned into a room rather close to the entrance hall and politely beckoned them to follow. Through the doors was a huge dining room with long dark wooden tables decorated with large flower centerpieces and the same glowing, golden candles. Golden draping also covered the walls, as the days dimming sunlight filtered through high arched windows. On one side of the room was a smaller table filled with trays of roast beef, five different salads, a large roasted chicken, three kinds of potatoes, three small cakes and a scrumptious looking trifle. Mrs. Smith gestured for them to help themselves, as Monty stood at the doorway behind her.

"Forgive me, but I must leave you now. Pressing issues of the house that I must attend to, you understand. Mr. Clearwater will now assume his duties as Master Huddleston's personal host. It was a pleasure meeting you both."

But before Mrs. Smith could walk away, Peter's father spoke up.

"Mrs. Smith, will Gillian be joining us?"

"Mistress Willowbrook, unfortunately, has been detained. She is, however, very much looking forward to meeting Master Huddleston and is delighted he has come to stay with her for the summer.

"Again, it was a pleasure."

And with that, Mrs. Smith scurried out of the dining room, meticulously consulting her silver clipboard. Monty, a cheerful expression lighting up his face, stepped up from the door.

"I will now be performing my hosting duties," he said happily. Then he left the room.

Peter and his father stood there for a few moments, not knowing what to do.

"Were we supposed to follow him?" asked Peter.

"I'm not sure," replied his father. "I suppose we should have something to eat."

Peter picked up one of the china plates and helped himself to roast beef and potatoes. Everything was absolutely delicious. They ate hungrily in silence, not realizing how starved they both were. It wasn't until after Peter's third helping of trifle that his father broke the silence.

"Its getting dark, I should be heading off soon."

Just then, Monty returned looking quite pleased with himself. Seeing that they were both through with their meal, he approached the table.

"Is there anything else I might offer you? Tea? Coffee?" asked Monty, excited at the prospect of bringing out even more refreshments.

"No thank you Monty, the food was delicious, but I should be getting on my way."

Peter started to feel nervous; he wanted his father to stay. Glancing at Peter, Monty continued...

"Will sir not be honoring us with his presence by allowing us to offer him a suite for the night?"

"No, no, I really must be going."

"Very well sir, allow me to escort you to your car."

Walking through the entrance hall and down the marble steps to the front of the manor, Monty stopped halfway toward their car, giving Peter and his father some privacy.

"It's been a pleasure to finally meet you sir, please do visit us again soon."

"Thank you Monty," said Peter's father, as he walked to his car.

"Now you behave Peter, I'll come back and get you at the end of the summer."

Peter said nothing, afraid of how it might come out of his suddenly timid vocal cords. He didn't want his father to leave.

"Take care of him, Monty."

"Of course, sir," said Monty, standing on the stairs and bowing slightly.

And with that, Peter's father got into his car, closed the door, and in a few minutes had almost reached the gates. Peter just stood there staring at the car until it slowly drove out of sight. He remained motionless for a few moments, until the heavy gray gates had closed again. Turning around, he saw Monty patiently waiting for him on the steps.

"Shall I show you to your room now, Master Huddleston?"

"Sure," said Peter quietly, "Monty?"

"Yes sir?"

"I'd like it if you just called me Peter...if you want."

"Thank you, sir."

Monty led Peter back up the marble stairs, through the high doors and passed the entrance hall into the long hallway.

"What are all these other rooms, Monty?" Peter asked, as they continued walking.

"That is the history museum, attended to by Madam Cornhen," said Monty, pointing to the doors across from the dining hall. "The library, headed by Mr. Frank, is over there," he continued, pointing to a pair of even larger doors at the end of the hall. "And beside it are the various private salons and parlors."

"You have a museum and a library in the house...um...manor?"

"Yes sir," said Monty happily, "We also have various gardens around the property that I think you'd enjoy."

Leading them away from the hall and up a pair of cream colored marble steps, Peter noticed even more crystal chandeliers, and more ledges filled with colorful flowers and golden candles. Moments later they entered another hall. It had a high ceiling and more large tapestries adorning the walls. Peter looked behind him and saw door, after door, after door, until the end of the hall vanished from sight.

"What are all these?"

"These are all mostly guest rooms, sir, but some are special function rooms."

"How many of these rooms are there?"

"Approximately three thousand."

"Three thousand!" said Peter, in a voice louder than he would have liked. "Who stays in them?"

"Most of them are vacant now," said Monty, "But we do get our busy seasons. Ah, here we are."

They had stopped at a corner of the hall. Peter turned and saw that the seemingly endless passage continued around the corner. Dominating the corner was a beautiful tapestry of an eagle right next to the door Monty was opening. Entering, Peter could hardly believe this was his room. It was huge, with two bedside tables on either side of a very large, very comfortable looking bed, with deep blue and cream-colored sheets. Moonlight was shining in through a wall of high arched windows that looked out onto a lush, green garden. A roaring fire was burning in an elegant fireplace across from an enormous oak desk. Next to the fireplace was another door that led off into a separate room. Peter noticed the old comic books from his suitcase were neatly stacked on a small cushioned bench at the end of his bed. There was also a round table in the center of the room that carried a large bowl of fresh assorted fruits, a silver tray of white chocolate truffles, and a large silver pitcher of cool water.

"This is amazing!" said Peter.

"Well thank you sir, I'm very happy to hear that," said Monty, a hint of relief in his voice. "This is your bed, I took the liberty of unpacking your clothes, that's your desk, some refreshments...and this is your washroom."

Peter followed Monty through the other door of the room and saw his bathroom. It was made from the same rich, cream marble, with a mountain of rolled up, fluffy blue towels forming a pyramid on a small round table in the center of the room. On one side of the chamber were the basin and mirrors and on the other side was a sparkling bath the size of a small swimming pool.

Walking back into the bedroom, Monty quickly glanced around to make sure everything was in order.

"And what time would you like breakfast brought up to you, sir? Is seven in the morning too early?"

"No, not at all," said Peter, as he admired his new abode.

"Splendid. After breakfast I would very much like to take you on a tour of the grounds. We could visit the animal preserve you've already found out about."

"Yeah, that sounds great!"

"Good, good, good," said Monty, seeming quite thrilled. "If you need anything, anything at all, please feel free to press the buzzer next to your bed." Monty pointed to a silver button on the wall, a few inches above Peter's bedside table. "Now that you are here, I'll let you settle in and..."

"Monty," said Peter, not meaning to interrupt him, "All this, the manor...what exactly does Aunt Gillian do?"

"Mistress Gillian is in the family business, sir, and I'm sure she will tell you all about it when she sees you tomorrow. She has been looking forward to meeting you for some time."

"I hope she's not expecting much."

"Whatever she is expecting, I'm sure you far surpass it." said Monty, beaming at him. "Goodnight, Peter."

"Goodnight, Monty," he answered, feeling a little more relieved.

Monty shut the door behind him, leaving Peter standing in the center of the room. After a few moments, he took off his leather book bag and tossed it on his new bed. Walking to the wardrobe, he put on his comfortable mismatched pajamas that were folded neatly on a shelf. After jumping into bed and pulling the rich blue and cream-colored sheets high around him, he continued to stare happily at his room. With libraries, animal preserves, dining halls, breakfast in bed, and this room, he realized things weren't going so badly after all. The summer was starting to look up.

As Peter drifted off to sleep, a small smile still etched on his face, others in the manor were impatiently stirring, furious that he had safely arrived.

✳ ✳ ✳

The next morning, Peter awoke, buried in a warm mountain of soft, fluffy pillows. He vividly recalled what a fantastic dream he'd had. He thought he'd be spending his summer in a tattered shack, wrestling vicious pet cats for rabbit meat. Yet, amazingly, he ended up in a beautiful mansion, with his own room and a jolly old butler. He slowly opened his eyes, hoping....

"Yes!" he yelled, as he sat up in bed.

The embers in the fireplace had long died, and the morning sun was starting to shine brightly through the wall of high arched windows near the bed. Peering outside, he viewed vast expanses of sprawling colorful gardens enclosed by a fence of high-walled bushes. He sprang off his comfy bed and hopped over to the small table in the center of the room, hungrily eying the silver tray of white chocolate truffles. Stuffing them exuberantly into his mouth, he had almost entirely devoured them when there was a knock at his door.

"Kurm-in," he said, through a mouthful of chocolate.

A mustachioed face slowly peeped into the room. Curious eyes glanced from the bed to the small table before the door swung open to reveal Monty, wearing the same pressed black suit and tie, holding a very large breakfast tray.

"Ah, good morning sir," he said jovially, "I see that you're already up, excellent!"

"Moring-Monee," said Peter, putting down the silver tray and trying to swallow.

"Ah yes, those truffles are quite delicious, aren't they? I prefer the raspberry filled ones myself," he continued, as he put the breakfast tray down on Peter's bed. "I say sir, those are very smart pajamas."

Peter looked down at his over sized, mismatched pajamas, and wondered what Monty was talking about.

"Uh, thanks,"

"I have my own smart parcels," said Monty cheerfully, "But you mustn't tell sir, not regulation with Mrs. Smith, you know."

Monty raised his pant legs to reveal two brightly colored, mismatched socks. One was checkered purple and yellow, and the other had happy faces all over it.

"What do you think, sir? Are they me?" asked Monty, a proud smile on his face.

"You know what Monty, I think they are," said Peter, grinning. The truth was, he thought those socks agreed with Monty much more than his pressed black suit did.

"Oh thank you sir, I quite think so too," said Monty, looking down at his beloved socks. "Now sir," he continued, turning to the tray, "I wasn't sure what you preferred, so I brought you cheese sandwiches."

"Huh?"

"Just kidding, sir!" said Monty brightly, "I brought a little of everything." Peter, looking down at the tray, saw small plates of ...well, everything. Pancakes, French toast, muffins, eggs, bacon, porridge, sausages, hashed browns, waffles, cereals and Danishes. There was also a steaming cup of tea. He couldn't wait to try it all.

"While you have breakfast, sir, I shall draw you a bath."

"Oh, no Monty, I could do it, that's alright,"

"Are you sure, sir? I'm quite good with a pen!" said Monty, clapping his hands together as he tossed back his head laughing hysterically. Peter couldn't help but chuckle. "Ha, ha, hee...a pen, a...sorry sir. Do indulge an old man," he continued, wiping away tears from his eyes.

"Very well sir, if you like, I could be back within the hour to begin our tour of the grounds."

"That sounds great" said Peter, sipping his hot tea. "Oh Monty, seeing as this is such a nice place, should, uh, is there anything specific I should wear?" he asked, glancing over at his rubber shoes and crumpled blue jeans, his boomerang still awkwardly sticking out of its pocket.

"Clothes I would think, sir," said Monty, who continued laughing madly to himself. Seeing Monty howling at his own joke caused Peter to nearly spit out his tea. Tearing furiously, Monty slowly managed to compose himself. "Sorry sir," he said, "I don't know what's gotten into me today. Mrs. Smith will think I've been in the brandy again. No, no, your usual attire will be just fine."

Monty left the room, still giggling under his own breath.

After his sumptuous breakfast and a warm bath, Peter felt as good as new. He got dressed and had just picked up his book bag when he heard a knock at the door.

"Come in Monty," he said, throwing the strap of his book bag across his chest. But there was no answer.

He started hearing the strangest sounds coming from the hallway, like gusts of wind were blowing in through an open window, then silence.

"Monty?" he repeated, half talking to himself. He walked over to the door and slowly opened it, looking down both ends of the corridor, but they were empty. He walked back to his bed and sat down. A few minutes later, he heard laughter coming from the hall, then a knock on his door.

"Come in, Monty," he said, recognizing the stifled giggling.

Monty entered, looking quite pleased to see him dressed and ready to go.

"Now, sir, I thought we'd take in a brief overview of the grounds today. You see, since Hillside Manor is very large, it will take quite a long time to see everything thoroughly. We can, however, visit the animal preserve in some detail. We probably won't be able to get through all of it, but at least you'll be able to see some of the animals we keep here,"

"Monty, will I still be meeting Aunt Gillian today?"

"Yes sir, Mistress Gillian informed me she wishes to see you some time after lunch."

"Oh, good," said Peter, feeling a little apprehensive at the thought of meeting his newly discovered aunt. But the excitement of seeing the rest of the manor allowed him to forget that feeling, and soon he and Monty were briskly walking down the corridor.

For the next few hours, Peter was amazed by the tour of the property. He knew the manor was big, but he never expected this. Monty had led him out onto the sprawling gardens, surrounded by high walled bushes. It seemed that after every path they followed, new surprises would pop up. First, they saw Willow Lake, which seemed even bigger than the one near Creamers and the lakeside shops. This lake seemed much deeper though, its still waters infinitely more dark and heavy. The greenery around the lake was wild and unkempt, as if no one ever came there, a far contrast to the rest of the tidy grounds.

Next to the lake was an aquarium, with huge glass tanks containing all sorts of fish Peter had never seen, including some that were very large, fanged and just plain mean looking. They descended several flights of metal steps into a large darkened underground chamber. Peter shivered from the cold that clung to the room, but was amazed by an entire wall of thick glass that looked directly into the depths of the lake, showing its mysterious, consuming waters. Peter could only see the intimidating darkness and a few small fish, but it was still incredible to be able to see that deeply into the lake.

Leaving the aquarium, Monty led him up winding paths to the top of a high hill, where they reached a large, constructed dome. As they got closer, Peter saw that the dome was teeming with thousands of birds of every size and shape imaginable. Large eagles perched on high, towering trees, and the surrounding air was filled with bluebirds and hawks flying side by side. Fat, round, red birds with orange beaks and little wings wobbled clumsily on thick branches, as tiny yellow birds fearlessly zoomed all around them, zigzagging in and out of the massive greenery.

Peter marveled at the sights and sounds of the menagerie, trying to count how many different birds there were until Monty led him back onto the winding path.

After climbing down the hill from the bird dome, more winding paths led them to a dry, dusty, clearing. The foliage had stopped growing, and the dirt floor was littered with huge, dense boulders. Monty told Peter they were in the manor's rock garden, and that toward the back, there was a rock maze made of high stone walls. Peter wanted to walk through it, but Monty insisted they make their way toward the animal preserve, as it was a rather long, confusing maze, and they had to be back in the manor for lunch.

After a pleasant stroll, they reached the animal preserve at last. Peter's first impression was that the preserve looked like a traditionally gated zoo. There were the usual bears, leopards and monkeys, but as they continued in even deeper, they found a lot of the animals weren't even caged at all. They were just lazily walking around, seemingly unaware that Peter and Monty were even there.

Of all the wonderful animals, Peter was especially taken, though at first completely terrified, by a powerful looking white tiger that had casually walked up to him...and licked him on the nose.

The tiger's name was Rune, and he was unusually friendly. He continued walking next to Peter and followed him wherever he went, leaving big paw marks on the ground. Peter loved petting the tame tiger and was surprised at how soft his fur was.

Monty suggested that they had better get going if they wished to see the flower gardens, which were right next door. Peter however, asked if they could continue to stay with the animals, opting to see the flower gardens some other time. It wasn't until early afternoon that they left the hospitable cat and started making their way back to the manor, the hot summer sun beating down on them.

"Rune seems to like you," said Monty, gladly. "He rarely lets people pet him."

"He's magnificent," said Peter. "I've never seen a white tiger. Is it safe to just let all the animals walk around like that? Don't they ever fight with each other?"

"Oh, no sir. They're terribly well fed and have been living here for a very long time. They're all quite tame...except of course for the hippos, they're vicious. But as long as you don't go into their pond, they keep to themselves."

They had almost reached the manor, when Peter casually got out his boomerang and was about to throw it.

"I say sir, what a marvelous looking contraption!" said Monty, curiously.

"Thanks, a friend gave it to me," said Peter, handing Monty his boomerang. He seemed fascinated by it, and was looking at it very closely.

"Yes, of course ..." he said, running his hand over the face of the boomerang. "Oak, if I'm not mistaken, sir."

"Yeah," said Peter, very impressed. "You wanna give it a go?"

"No sir, I couldn't possibly," he said, handing the boomerang back.

"You sure? Okay." Peter raised back his arm and threw the boomerang into the air, sending it racing high up into the clear blue sky.

"Good show, sir," said Monty, gazing upward "Oh my, it's...it's coming back ...it's... DIVE FOR COVER!"

Peter caught his boomerang, just as Monty dove for the ground.

"Monty? Monty, it's alright, I caught it," said Peter, trying very hard not to laugh.

"Ah, yes, sir, of course. So sorry, don't know what came over me," he responded, calmly brushing off his suit, and turning bright red.

"You knew it was going to come back, right?"

"Yes, of course, sir...boomerang...well, we best be getting off to lunch."

Peter was very hungry by the time they reached the dining hall. A buffet was already set on the same table that he and his father had eaten from the day before. He was helping himself to fried chicken and potatoes, when he noticed Monty standing at the dining hall door.

"Aren't you going to have lunch, Monty?"

"Please go right ahead, sir. Although I would like to, it wouldn't be proper conduct as a house host."

"Well alright, if you're sure," said Peter, sitting down at the table.

"Yes, sir."

"Monty?" he asked, through a mouthful of potato, "How come there's nobody in the halls, or anywhere else? It must take a lot of people to run this place, but I hardly see anyone."

"The custom of the house is that the staff tends to the manor in secret, mostly late at night, so as not to clutter the halls and cause disturbance to our guests. I assure you, we have quite a large staff here," he said proudly.

"They must be really busy taking care of all those rooms."

"Yes sir, I'm sure they are. Mrs. Smith does an excellent job organizing everyone. For instance, she personally saw to the arranging of your room and supervises its cleaning."

"Oh," said Peter, standing up to help himself to more chicken. "She must have been the one who knocked on my door this morning." He sat down and was about to take a big bite, when he noticed that Monty's demeanor had drastically changed. The cheerful expression on his face had vanished. He looked utterly aghast.

"Someone knocked on your door, sir?" asked Monty, very carefully.

"Uh, yeah," said Peter. "I thought it was you coming to pick me up for our tour, but when I said to come in, no one answered. Monty, what's wrong?"

Monty looked shocked.

"Then what happened, sir?"

"Then, um, I went to see who it was but no one was in the hall..."

"Is that everything sir, nothing else happened?" he asked, hanging on Peter's every word.

"Yeah, that's it."

Monty looked as if a hundred thoughts were running through his head. Then Peter remembered something.

"Oh, yeah...well, maybe I imagined it, but there was this noise after the knocks, like wind or something."

That did it. Monty looked like he was about to pass out. The blood suddenly rushed from his face.

"Sir," he said, in a very controlled voice, "There is a button under the corner of the table top where you are sitting. Would you press it?"

"Uh, sure," said Peter. Putting down his fork and feeling under the table with his hands, he found a small button and pressed it.

"Monty, is something wrong?"

In moments, Peter heard rushed footsteps coming from down the hall. Monty stepped out, and soon Mrs. Smith walked briskly up to him, still carrying her silver clipboard. This did not look good. Had he committed some error toward her when she came to supervise the cleaning of his room? Did he insult her in some way? Was that possible considering he didn't even do anything?

For a few tense moments, Monty and Mrs. Smith continued speaking to each other in hurried whispers. Mrs. Smith had placed her hand nervously to her chest. Afterwards, she quickly walked up to Peter, with Monty still waiting in the hall.

"Master Huddleston, come with me. The time has come to meet your aunt."

4

MEETING GILLIAN

Peter didn't know what to think. Something strange was definitely happening. They were all walking hurriedly down the hall, Mrs. Smith and Monty on either side of him. Both looked very serious and neither one said a word. They had walked up the stairs to the corridor where Peter's room was, and for a while he thought that might be where they were going. Instead of turning right towards his room, they turned left and bustled down the seemingly endless passageway. They stopped at an arched door next to a large tapestry of a black panther resting near a tree. Mrs. Smith pulled out a small gold key from the breast pocket of her blazer and unlocked the heavy door, and they entered a large room, about the same size as Peter's, furnished with chairs and tables draped in blue and gold. There were no windows, and the overall look of the chamber was very formal. One other set of high arched doors stood across the room from where they had just entered. Monty led Peter to a cushioned chair and gestured for him to sit down. Meanwhile, Mrs. Smith locked the door behind them, walked across the room, and exited through the high arched doors.

A few moments had passed in silence, when Peter noticed Monty was straightening his suit and flattening his tie, a distinct air of solemnity washing over his face. Just then, the high arched doors opened. Mrs. Smith had one hand on each door and had slowly pulled them apart and stepped off to the right, standing unusually straight, with her hands at her side.

A second woman walked into the room. She was the most beautiful woman Peter had ever seen. She was very tall and wore a golden gown in the style of an ancient French aristocrat, except more simple and light. Across her chest, from her shoulder to her waist, was a deep blue sash. On it, below the shoulder, was pinned a single golden medal. On her side, near her waist, was what seemed to be a coil of thin, golden rope. She was fair skinned, and her long, wavy hair was loosely pulled back and fell naturally to her shoulders. Her hair was the color of caramel.

She carried herself with an air of dignity and repose Peter had never seen before. Her face was kind, yet resolute. When she saw Peter, she smiled at him warmly. She looked to Monty, who quickly walked up to her and gave a slight bow. As they talked quietly, Mrs. Smith closed the high arched doors behind them and stood at attention. Monty pulled up a chair in front of Peter, and then left quickly with Mrs. Smith through the front door and out of the room.

Peter heard Mrs. Smith locking the door from outside, as the gowned woman elegantly sat down in front of him. She was still smiling warmly and was looking at him reassuringly. Peter gazed at her in awe. Even though he could see her eyes were green and not blue, he still couldn't believe how much she looked like his mother. Reaching out and gently touching his hand, she began to speak.

"Hello Peter," she said in a gentle voice. "I'm so happy to finally meet you. My name is Gillian."

"Y-you're my aunt," he stuttered.

"And you're my nephew," she said, beaming at him. "It's amazing how much you look like Patricia,"

"You look like her, too,"

"Thank you. That's quite a compliment,"

For the next few moments, Peter and his aunt just looked at each other. Then slowly, he started to feel an ache in the pit of his stomach. Despite himself, he felt his throat tighten.

"Y-you look so much like her," he said in a whisper.

She nodded slowly, and again placed her hand gently on top of his. Composing himself, Peter tried to think of something to say.

"I like your house," he said, managing a smile.

"Thank you, I hope your room is comfortable. Fredericka fixed it especially for you."

"Fredericka? Oh, Mrs. Smith. Yes. I like my room a lot. Um..." he started, feeling this topic should be addressed. "I hope I didn't offend her or anything."

"Of course not, why would you think that?"

"Well, Monty seemed concerned when I told him she knocked on my door. He said Mrs. Smith supervises my room being cleaned."

Aunt Gillian looked at him momentarily, her eyes smiled as she spoke.

"I'm sure you haven't offended Mrs. Smith. She's very happy you're here, and Montgomery is positively thrilled."

"Yeah, Monty's been really cool!"

"I'm sure he has. He tells me you've already seen some of the grounds."

"Oh yeah, they were great! We went to see the animals, the rock garden, that bird dome thing, and the lake. I wish I had a lake in my house!"

"I use to enjoy the lake as well. It's been a while since I've even seen it."

"Oh, it's really nice," he said enthusiastically.

"And your father, I hope he's well."

"Dad? Yeah, he's fine. He wanted to see you before he left. He drove me here."

"I was hoping to see him as well. I'm sorry I wasn't able to. I had some meetings I couldn't miss."

"Oh, that's alright," he said, not meaning to make her apologize. "We had supper together. He really liked the manor, too."

"I'm so glad. I wish he could have stayed the night. It would have been so nice to catch up with him today."

Peter was very taken aback. He felt oddly comfortable with his aunt, even if they had only just met. Not only was she not a crazy woman with blue hair who owned hundreds of cats, but she didn't seem to be at odds with his father at all. In fact, she sounded very sincere in wanting to see him.

As his hand rested on top of the book bag on his lap, he felt the hard edge of the small framed photograph he had of his parents. Although he was surprised at the fondness his aunt showed for them, he was still curious to see how she'd respond to his most prized possession.

"I've been carrying an old photograph around with me, it's a really good one, I think you might like it," he said, pulling the frame out of his bag and handing it to his aunt. She took it carefully in her hands.

For a few moments, she looked at it closely, her eyes misting slightly.

"Yes, I remember Patricia telling me about when they carved their initials in that tree...look at her laughing. She had the most wonderful laugh. She always made everyone in the room start laughing with her, even if they didn't know why."

Peter hung on her every word. Except for a few kind words from the Twickeypoos, no one had ever really spoken about his mother before.

"What was she like?" he asked earnestly.

"Your mother? Well...Patricia was such a joy. She was very funny, very smart, and very protective. She and I used to run around the manor on all these little adventures. We had a pet white tiger, his name was ..."

"Rune!" yelled Peter loudly.

"Yes! Oh, you've met Rune?" she shouted, sounding delighted. "Isn't he fantastic? We used to smuggle him into the manor! He was a small cub then. We'd hide him under our bed pillows and play with him in our rooms. We were all so young. Your mother was a ball of energy, and very brave...yes, Patricia was very brave. It was so hard to be away from her when we were older."

"So you and mom got along?"

"Of course," she said warmly. "I loved your mother very much. One of the hardest things I've ever had to do was being separated from her for so long. We were sisters, and we were friends. Being separated from each other was a sacrifice we hated having to make."

"Why did you have to separate? Was...was it because of dad?"

"What? No...no...It had nothing to do with your father. He and I never really got to know each other. Patricia and I could still keep in touch when they first met. I suppose it makes sense that he would think your mother and I didn't get along well, hardly seeing each other for so long. But she and I made the right decision. It was for the best."

"But why?"

Aunt Gillian slightly settled herself in her chair.

"I don't suppose your father told you what duties I have here at Hillside. No, I doubt Patricia ever told him herself. I'm a kind of politician here."

"What kind of politician?"

"I handle the affairs of a place called Galadria."

"Are we in Galadria now?" he asked curiously, remembering the empty, barren land he rode through to get to the manor.

"Well," she continued, "The manor is considered Galadrian soil, but Galadria itself is close by."

He could see his aunt thinking very carefully.

"Peter," she said seriously, "Galadria is part of the reason I've asked you to Hillside. It's very important and I need you to listen carefully."

"Okay," he said, leaning in slightly from his chair. And what did she mean by her 'asking him' to Hillside? He thought his father decided to send him here.

"My Galadrian duties are quite important and were given to me when I was very young. You see, I must devote a lot of time to my work there. That's the reason your mother and I were separated so often."

"Alright."

"Things are done differently in Galadria. The politicians are required to announce who will further help them in their duties, and that's what I've come to ask you. As my sister's son, you have a right to help me with my work. Of course, it's entirely your choice, but because of present circumstances I would need to know your decision soon."

"Well...I'm not sure what you mean," he said truthfully.

Placing Peter's framed photograph gently on her lap, she proceeded to unbuckle the round golden medal on her sash and handed it to him. Looking at it, he saw it had an embossed crest on it, two scepters crossed over each other with four stars forming a semicircle above them. The medal was exquisitely made and very heavy.

"This is the Galadrian crest," she said.

"It's beautiful,"

"What I'm going to say may be difficult to hear, but there's no other way to say it. All I ask is that you let me finish, and regardless of your decision, you keep what I am about to tell you to yourself."

"Okay," he said tentatively.

"Your mother and I are from the House of Willowbrook, hence our last name. Our family has always had a special commitment to Galadria. The reason you and I have never met is because I told your father it would be better that way. I wanted you to have as much of a normal life as possible until you were old enough to understand.

"I think that's why your father has been upset with me. I know he wanted me to have a bigger role in your life after your mother passed away, and he couldn't understand why I wasn't. I don't think he has forgiven me for "abandoning" you. There was no way I could tell him about the reality of things, especially in his grief," Gillian explained quietly. "As much as I wanted to..."

Peter watched his aunt solemnly; he could feel how serious, how important, this conversation was to her. And the heaviness of her tone prickled at his feelings.

After a moment, she continued.

"I have no children, I'm not able to, and your mother was my only sibling. Recent events in Galadria have forced me to name who will follow me in my work. I held it off for as long as I could. I didn't want to have to reveal this to you until you were older, but now I have no choice. You are my only nephew, and are my natural successor to Galadria."

"Uh-huh," said Peter, his mouth hanging open.

He could not believe the turn this had taken. Everything was going so well. He was the what? To the who? To the where? To the what? Then a thought dawned on him.

He was right. His aunt was stark raving mad!

"Peter? ...Peter?"

"Uh-huh," he said, his mouth still open.

Sure she was rich, and alright, everyone in the manor did seem to agree with what she was saying, and he did see the grounds, but...but ...

"Peter?"

"Uh-huh."

"I think you'd better come with me."

She handed him back his framed photograph, which slipped from his numb fingers. Peter snapped out of his shock for a moment, desperately reaching out for his prized picture, but not before Aunt Gillian, with lightning reflexes, grabbed the falling frame and carefully handed it back to her nephew. Moving in slow motion, he put the frame into his bag.

Aunt Gillian stood up and gently took his hand; she led him through the high arched doors she had entered from. Hand in hand they walked down a small hall and into a huge, circular chamber that had a very high, domed ceiling. Polished tables and benches followed the darkened circular shape of the room, all in levels receding onto the chamber floor. Peter thought it looked like something from the United Nations, except that at the center of the floor was a large, elaborate, golden throne. Hanging against the wall behind it were two huge crisscrossed blue and gold scepters, with four golden stars above them, forming a semi-circle. The wall hangings matched exactly the crest that was on the medal in his hand.

"I...don't know..." he started, but couldn't find the words to continue.

"This is the Galadrian Council Room. In Galadria, I am Queen Gillian of the Noble House of Willowbrook, Supreme Ruler of the Realm. And you, Peter, are not only Peter Huddleston, you are Peter Willowbrook Huddleston, son of Patricia Willowbrook and heir to the Galadrian throne."

Peter let out a small whimpering noise and felt himself getting dizzy.

Aunt Gillian strengthened her grip on his hand as she led him to one of the polished benches. He sat down and stared at the medal he was holding. His aunt sat beside him.

"Peter, there's more," she said, still grasping his hand.

"More?" he asked, impossibly.

"This is a pivotal time in Galadria's history. You are the only lineage connected to me, but because of your youth and absence from Galadria, someone has challenged your position to the throne. His name is Knor, of the House of Shadowray. He is the eldest son in a noble family that has tried to destroy the House of Willowbrook for centuries. He also would be my legal successor if I have not named an heir. He's challenging that unless I can present my successor to the Supreme Council, the monarchy is unstable and Galadria's future is at risk. He will insist on taking my place, citing that his own many siblings are his ready and able successors," Aunt Gillian said, staring intently at the golden throne.

She slowly turned her face back to Peter and took his other hand in hers.

"For now, my position is secure and I have the backing of the council, but unless I can provide an heir, Knor will not rest, and Galadria will be in danger. The members of the House of Shadowray are fanatics, violent and known for their cruelty. Knor, and the House of Shadowray, gaining the crown would throw our peaceful realm into utter chaos. I am certain the other noble families would refuse to accept his ascension. There would be war waged against the new monarchy. A civil war...such battles between the opposing political factions would tear our populace apart. All who opposed the House of Shadowray would be eliminated, order would be lost and countless lives would be destroyed. I know the people of Galadria; they would fight, but against Shadowray and their supporters, too much would be lost.

"I'm asking you to be publicly and officially named as my successor. You are my rightful heir, and, though he would wish to, Knor cannot dispute that.

"You would have no official duties until you were a fully-grown adult. You would finish school and live with your father, but in the summers could come to Hillside and learn about Galadria and our people. And as you grow up I will be able to use the time to dismantle the House of Shadowray and banish Knor. By the time I step down, you would be a grown man, distinguished in years and ready to take your place. I didn't want to have to ask this of you until you were much older, but Knor has left me no choice," his aunt said, her voice low and insistent.

"There must be someone else," he whispered breathlessly, feeling overwhelmed by the insanity of her story.

"In the laws of succession, only a child of noble birth can succeed the throne. I'm not able to have children, and you are the only child of my only sister."

Peter was speechless. He had no idea what to say, what to even think. He was just a kid from a small neighborhood who hardly talked to anyone. He threw a boomerang around. He wasn't a noble! He wasn't even the top student in his class! He stared at his aunt wishing this wasn't true, but knowing it was. His mind was churning, but words would not come to mind.

Finally, unable to think of anything else, he whispered, "What's Galadria like?"

Seeing the panic and confusion on his face, his aunt lightened her tone.

"It's beautiful. Galadria is known as the Golden Realm. Most of our people are peaceful and happy, our way of life is simple."

"Why is it called the Golden Realm?" he asked limply.

"Because Galadria and her people are fortunate. It is a very prosperous land, and the people have faired well," she said happily. "And because whenever the sun rises or sets, the cities are engulfed in a rich, golden light that transforms most everything it touches."

"Oh..."

"Peter, what I ask of you is no small thing. But there is no time. Knor has already swayed the Supreme Council to have second thoughts about the validity of his claim," she said, settling her eyes on his with an expectant look. Aunt Gillian sat even straighter on the bench, and took a deep breath.

"I ask you to agree to a life of great privilege and great responsibility. You would not be expected to rule or make decisions in any capacity until I step down from the throne...which will not happen until I am a very old woman," she added with a wink.

"Until then, what would I do?" he asked wonderingly.

"You would be formally presented to the council, and would spend your summers at Hillside learning about Galadria and spending your time on the grounds. There would also, of course, be the occasional ceremony to introduce you to the rest of the nobles, but those events are also held here at the manor. Then when you came of age, you would go through the traditional 'Rights of Passage,' a series of challenges that the rulers of Galadria must pass, as I did, to prove your readiness and ability to the council."

"And what if I choose not to accept?" he asked.

"Then you would go back to your previous life and everything would return to normal."

"But how about you?"

Aunt Gillian smiled gently and seemed genuinely touched by his concern.

"I would be fine. I would continue my reign over Galadria, and Willowbrook's struggle against Shadowray would continue. We would find a way to prosper."

"How? You said I was your only heir."

"Yes," she said. "You are. But this is your choice and yours alone. Yours...no one has expectations for you to decide one way or another. I simply present an option that is yours through birthright. Whether you choose to take it or not is up to you."

"But we wouldn't get to see each other?"

"We would," she said slowly, "But not often. I'm afraid your presence here is a threat to Knor, and until I have control over him, the manor would not be secure. Only a few select trusted people know where you and your father live, it's much safer for you there."

"But if I stayed, wouldn't it be more dangerous?"

"Once you have been officially presented to the council, Knor has lost. There would be no reason for his presence here at Hillside, or near the council. You see, Knor himself poses no real threat to me, except that after you, he is the next in line to the throne. When my successor is named, I remain Queen and Ruler. Knor, with no real title or power, will have no reason to be here. And if he makes even a shred of trouble, I can deal with him as a ruling queen. However, as long as he abides by the rules, I must address his accusations."

Peter's head was swimming. He was putting in enormous amounts of energy just trying not to pass out.

"Aunt Gillian, I don't know what to say. This is so hard to believe, much less understand. One minute I have no relatives at all, and the next thing I know, my long lost aunt, who by the way is a ruling queen, is telling me I'm heir to her throne. I...I need some time."

He slowly handed Aunt Gillian back her golden medal. She took it gently with one hand, and gave his hand a gentle squeeze with the other.

"Of course," she said warmly. "Just know I will support you fully in whatever choice you make."

After buckling her medal to her sash, she leaned in and embraced him. Peter could not remember the last time he was hugged.

"I'm so happy we've finally gotten to meet," she said, smiling at him. "I am sorry that it is under such urgent circumstances."

Just then, Mrs. Smith and Monty entered, bowed, and silently stood at attention on either side of the high arched doors. Aunt Gillian glanced over at Mrs. Smith, who nodded to her.

"I must go now," said Aunt Gillian regretfully. "I shouldn't leave the council for too long. We shall see each other again tomorrow."

She was about to rise, when she glanced over at Monty and sat herself back down.

"Montgomery tells me someone knocked on your door this morning. The way Hillside is run, only me, Mrs. Smith, Montgomery and two other members of the staff know where you are. They have each assured me none of them did it. Not only is it against house rules, it is a breach of protocol to visit you unannounced, especially when you are alone. Hillside Manor has its own defenses, and the room you are in is a special one. However, until further notice, please do not go anywhere in the manor without Montgomery, and if someone knocks unexpectedly on your door again, do not answer it, and press the buzzer next to your bed. Do you understand?"

"Yes," Peter answered. "Do you think it could have been Knor?"

"I don't see how," she said, a bit too quickly. "Beyond these doors, no member of the council or any other official is able to pass unless specifically invited. The House of Willowbrook owns Hillside Manor, and even Knor would not be foolish enough to trespass. However, I would prefer it if you stayed near Montgomery. He's not only your host here, he's also your guardian."

Peter looked over at Monty, who gave him a small nod.

"Now I must go," she continued." Montgomery will escort you to your room."

Peter stood up with his aunt, who was looking at him intently. Then she did something he did not expect. She placed her hands gently on top of his shoulders and did a small, very slow, deliberate curtsy, while slightly bowing her head.

"Until tomorrow," she said warmly.

And with that, Aunt Gillian glided through another set of high arched doors. Mrs. Smith followed quickly behind her. It was only when they had gone that Monty moved towards him.

"Come sir," he said, "We should go."

Minutes later, Peter and Monty quietly walked through the manor's elegant halls towards his room. Peter was trying to wrap his mind around everything his aunt had said to him. As he tried to remember everything his aunt told him, and deal with the shock of her revelations, he shook his head as he recalled his aunt's parting.

"Monty," he asked curiously, "why did Aunt Gillian perform that little curtsy toward me before she left the room?"

"That sir is called a Renlo. It is a Galadrian gesture that shows that the person giving it has the deepest sense of respect for you. It is considered sacred and of great significance. To my knowledge, Mistress Gillian has only performed the Renlo to one other person."

"Who?" he asked

"Your mother."

✳ ✳ ✳

Peter spent the rest of the day in his room, on his bed, lost in thought, considering the situation that had been presented to him. Although it was hard to accept, the reality of Hillside was starting to sink in. At Monty's insistence, he would be having dinner in his room that night. It wasn't until he heard him knocking on the door that he realized he'd been sitting motionless for hours.

"It's me, sir," said Monty, entering slowly. He was carrying a large dinner tray and sounded almost apologetic to be interrupting. Peter was glad to see him.

"Hi Monty," he said, trying to sound cheerful.

"Hello," he replied, glad to hear Peter's tone was not glum. "For dinner tonight we've made a lovely roast beef, a fresh green salad, a wonderful plate of assorted cheeses, and for dessert...a great big, hot fudge, banana split sundae with dollops of whipped cream. It always helps me think."

Monty gingerly placed the dinner tray on the bed, next to Peter. Walking over to the fireplace, he proceeded to stack several thick logs snugly into it, and soon, a blazing fire filled the room with a cozy, reassuring warmth.

"Enjoy, sir," said Monty happily. "I'll be back shortly to collect your tray. Breakfast will be at the same time tomorrow, and I have been informed that you will be meeting Mistress Gillian directly after lunch."

Monty started to walk briskly towards the door.

"Monty wait, I wanted to ask you... I mean, you must know about all this, what do you think?"

"It really isn't my place to comment, sir. This is your choice. I have no right to influence it either way."

"But...me! A future...ruler! That's crazy! I can't even imagine what that would take! I'm not the kind of person who could do this!"

"All I can say, sir," he started, "Is that Mistress Gillian is one of the finest rulers Galadria has ever known. Her reign is a testament to both incredible strength and unwavering determination. Qualities members of the Willowbrook House are famous for. Your mother had those same qualities, as do you, whether you are aware of them or not. It is not only your choice, but your inherent right to use those attributes, either in Galadria or wherever else you choose to go."

When Monty returned to collect his dinner tray, Peter was sitting up in bed, a virtual statue in mismatched pajamas. He had eaten his entire dinner, all the chocolate bars in his bag, the bowl of fruit, as well as the refilled silver tray of white chocolate truffles in the center of the room. Peter didn't even notice Monty he was so trapped in his thoughts.

A brief respite into sleep did not last long and soon he was awake again. It was still dark when he had climbed out of bed and constructed another blaze in the fireplace, mesmerized by its crackling, flickering flames. A million times a million thoughts were racing through his head, though he found himself much calmer, and open to the possibilities behind them. By the time the sun had started to rise, he had made his decision. When Monty entered with his breakfast tray, he was still sitting in front of the fireplace, watching the last glowing embers slowly, but inevitably, die out. He asked Monty if he could spend the day in his room and have his lunch brought up to him.

The rest of the morning, Peter systematically rethought his decision, making sure over and over again that he was making the right choice. He got dressed, strapped his book bag firmly across his chest, and ate a good lunch. Patiently waiting on his bed, he watched as Monty quietly stepped inside.

"Sir, I hope you're ready. Mistress Gillian is waiting for you."

5

NEGOTIATIONS

Peter followed Monty down the hall from his room. They eventually reached the tapestry of the black panther resting near a tree. Standing next to it was Mrs. Smith, firmly anchored to her silver clipboard.

"Good afternoon, Master Huddleston," she said politely.

"Good afternoon," he said, managing a smile.

Mrs. Smith reached in the breast pocket of her blazer and pulled out the small gold key.

Peter entered the same formal sitting room and saw his aunt sitting on a chair, patiently waiting for him. She was wearing the same light golden gown and medaled blue sash. Monty and Mrs. Smith gave her a small bow and exited the room again, closing the door behind them. When Peter turned back towards his aunt, she was observing him warmly.

"Aunt Gillian," he said determinedly, "I've made my decision. I thought about it well and considered everything you said...yeah... yes, I accept."

Aunt Gillian seemed taken aback. He could tell she did not expect him to make his decision so soon.

"Peter," she said in a concerned voice, "Are you absolutely sure? Don't do it to please me. It must be for yourself."

"I'm sure," he said confidently. "When I got over the initial shock of everything, I realized I'd have to be crazy to turn this down! The chance to help all those people! I never felt that I fit in where I live now, not in school, not at home. But here, in a strange way, I feel that I do. I know it won't be easy, but like you said, I have a really long time to learn about Galadria before I have to do anything official. And you'll be here the whole time to help me if I need it. Besides, I'll still see dad, just not for the summers. Galadria seems to need me, and...Well, no one's ever seemed to really need me before. So, yes, I accept."

Aunt Gillian leaped up and threw her arms around him.

"Are you sure?" she asked seriously, still hugging him rather tightly. "Do you need more time to think about it? This isn't something you can change your mind about later. You must be sure you're sure."

"Yes, Aunt Gillian," he answered, straining for breath.

"Oh Peter, I'm so happy," she said exuberantly, her eyes beaming. "And I promise you, I will do everything in my power to make sure you have every opportunity and resource you need to learn about our customs and way of life. Your care and well being will be my highest concern."

"So...I guess I'm a Willowbrook now," he said, his aunt releasing him from her embrace.

"You've always been a Willowbrook," she offered, reassuringly.

"Oh yeah," he blushed, "That's right."

Faint sobs became increasingly audible from the hall outside.

"Shall we tell them the good news?" she asked excitedly.

Peter nodded.

"Fredericka, Montgomery, please come in."

Monty and Mrs. Smith entered and closed the door behind them. They both stood stiffly at attention. Monty's eyes were slightly tearing.

"Peter has dutifully accepted our offer. He is going to take his place as the next Willowbrook successor."

Mrs. Smith smiled broadly. Monty burst into tears.

"Fredericka, Montgomery," continued Aunt Gillian decisively, "Please make the necessary arrangements. Peter will need to start his schedule at once. I will alert the council of his decision. He will need to be briefed on protocol. Unfortunately we won't be able to fit a formal costume, time is of the essence."

"Will I be meeting the council soon?" Peter asked.

"Yes, as soon as possible. The sooner you're presented to the council, the sooner your place here is secured. Knor will have no reason to stay here, and will have to leave. All you'll have to do is sit next to me in the council room. I'll introduce you to the council, and you'll be presented with the official Galadrian 'Lorna,' it looks like a globe of the Willowbrook family tree. Once you sign it

"'Peter Willowbrook Huddleston,' the presentation is complete."

The next few hours were rushed. Aunt Gillian sped off to the council room, with Mrs. Smith directly behind her, scribbling frantically on her silver clipboard. Monty led Peter back to his room, still wiping the tears from his eyes. The two of them began the arduous task of going through Peter's minimal wardrobe. Monty finally settled on a dark blue, long sleeved, collared shirt. Peter changed quickly, tucked his shirt into his trousers, and slung his leather book bag across his chest. Monty tried to convince him to leave his bag, but Peter wanted it, as well as his boomerang, with him, insisting it made him feel more at ease.

With Peter's attire taken care of, Monty further instructed him on how the presentation would unfold. It was just like Aunt Gillian had said. He would enter with her, sit at her side, and sign the Lorna. He would not be expected to say anything, and shouldn't, unless his aunt expressly bid him to do so. After the signing, he would bow to Aunt Gillian, then to the council, and both of them would exit the same way they came in.

They had just gone over it for the fifth time, when they heard a quick knock at the door. Mrs. Smith hurriedly entered.

"Are you ready, Master Huddleston?" she asked.

"Yes," he said, after glancing at Monty, who was nodding to him.

"Splendid. The council is assembled."

Mrs. Smith led Peter and Monty down the hall to the same formal room they had just been in. As they entered, Peter saw his aunt standing in front of the great arched doors. She was dressed in her light golden gown and deep blue sash, but as she turned, he saw she was wearing a jeweled gold band across her forehead. He assumed it was the equivalent of a Galadrian crown. Monty and Mrs. Smith performed their obligatory bows, and positioned themselves to open the great, arched doors.

"Are you ready?" Aunt Gillian asked, confidently.

Peter nodded.

They proceeded through to the small hall just before the council room.

"Remember," said Aunt Gillian calmly, "Just sign the Lorna, Peter Willowbrook Huddleston, and the presentation is complete. The council will be to your right, they're the group of twelve wearing purple robes."

Peter took a deep breath, as Aunt Gillian nodded to Mrs. Smith and Monty. They slowly pulled open the high doors to the shadowed council room. Peter froze. The huge, domed chamber was completely filled with people. He saw the lighted Galadrian crest, and before it, the large gold throne, with a smaller golden chair to its right. Standing at attention on either side of the chairs, were eight intimidating guards in shining, golden armor.

A guard wearing a scarlet cloak stepped forward and raised his hand to quiet the room.

"Ladies and gentlemen of the court," he loudly proclaimed, "It is my great honor to present to you, Her Royal Majesty, Queen Gillian of the Noble House of Willowbrook, Supreme Ruler of the Realm of Galadria."

The entire room stood to see Aunt Gillian and Peter standing at the doorway. Peter looked up at his aunt, as she ever so slightly nodded her head. They walked carefully down the steps toward the throne, the sea of people on either side of them bowing as they passed. Everyone was very formally dressed, most of the women wore gowns, and many of the men wore ornamented, buttoned up coats. Some of the assembled were adorned with an assortment of medals, and had various sashes draped across their chests.

The eight golden guards bowed deeply as Aunt Gillian approached her throne. Peter followed suit, and took his place in front of the smaller chair beside her. As they simultaneously sat down, the rest of the room noisily took their seats, leaving the eight armored guards standing at the ready. Peter looked to his right and came face to face with the Supreme Council. They were a group of six men and six women, draped in robes of deep purple. Each of them was looking at him with great interest. In fact, everyone in the room was looking at him with great interest. Peter's gaze settled on a tall, foreboding man to the left of the throne, standing directly across from the council. He was wearing a black, hooded cloak and had a dark mustache and goatee. Like a vulture perched behind a golden podium, he was the only other person in the room left standing.

"Ladies and gentlemen of the court," started Aunt Gillian, her voice sure and full. "Thank you for attending on such short notice. As we are all well aware, Knor, of the Noble House of Shadowray, has challenged me to name my successor. It is Knor's right to do so, not only for the stability of the monarchy, but also for the future security of our golden realm. It is with this future in mind, that I have invited you to this very momentous occasion. Sitting to my right is the future of the monarchy. Ladies and gentlemen of the court, respected members of the ruling noble families, and esteemed members of the Supreme Council, it is with great pride that I present to you, Peter Willowbrook Huddleston, son of my lovingly departed sister, Patricia Willowbrook, and rightful heir to the Galadrian throne."

Without hesitation, applause filled the chamber. Several people had risen to their feet, and Peter was surprised that everyone seemed thrilled by the announcement, everyone except the cloaked man standing ominously behind the podium. And the council had not reacted either way to this announcement. They all turned in unison, stoically facing him, eerily assessing him with a palpable indifference.

Once the applause had died down and everyone had taken their seats, one of the council members stood up. He was an elderly man with silver hair, who possessed an undeniable air of authority.

"Your Majesty," he said, speaking directly to Aunt Gillian, "Has the successor knowingly agreed to this future?"

"Yes, Lord Grandon," answered Aunt Gillian respectfully. "He has."

"Then unless Knor, of the Noble House of Shadowray, has any further objection, this council accepts the royal successor as being a true son of the House of Willowbrook, and is ready to proceed with the official signing of the Lorna."

A black haired woman next to Lord Grandon slowly stood up, holding a glowing, golden sphere, the size of a globe.

"Wait," said a deep, dark voice from Peter's left. He turned to see the cloaked man with the goatee glaring at him.

"Yes, Knor of Shadowray," said Lord Grandon.

Ahhh... Knor, Peter thought.

"May I make one last address to the council?" said Knor roughly, his deep voice echoing strength.

"You may," said Lord Grandon unaffectedly, as he sat down. Peter looked up and saw Aunt Gillian calmly facing Knor. Knor spoke directly to the council, his hooded cloak throwing his face in and out of shadow.

"Esteemed members of the Supreme Council, the named successor is obviously a valid member of the House of Willowbrook. With him, the stability of the Willowbrook monarchy is secured...

"Or is it? I ask the council why it has taken so long for her Majesty to bring about her successor. Where did he come from? Because I assure you, he has never lived or breathed in our golden realm. In fact, I dare say, there was such a rush to get him here today, that he, our future monarch, is not even garbed in Galadrian cloth."

Aunt Gillian wasn't taking her eyes off Knor. He, on the other hand, never made eye contact with her, and continued to look only at the council.

"I wonder," said Knor maliciously, "if the successor has any basic knowledge of Galadria at all. Her Majesty has stated how he is our future, yet how can he be if he knows nothing of our past, has never stepped foot in Galadria itself? In fact, my sources tell me this child is a menace in the village he lives in, having physically attacked both his relatives and neighbors. Yes, he is the son of Patricia Willowbrook, but he has not benefited from her guidance or influence since he was an infant."

Peter began to feel a swell of resentment and anger rising in him. He did not like Knor at all. How did he know about Aunt Celeste and Mrs. Crewpot? And how dare he use his mother's name against him.

"So I ask you, ladies and gentlemen of the council, are we to divulge our deepest, most sacred secrets to this unknown boy? Are we to give him such an unrivaled position of power so freely? I think not. But, alas, despite his sordid history, royal blood does flow through his veins, as the esteemed council has pointed out. However, I must ask the council to safeguard our future and the future of Galadria. I challenge the successor to undergo the Rites of Passage. If he truly is as ready and capable as her Majesty assures us he is, then he has no reason to refuse. If he does not accept, then I shudder to think at how easily and precipitously we give access to our most sacred throne."

Peter could tell Aunt Gillian hadn't expected this. Knor's challenge had seemed to reach the sensibilities of the council. They were whispering quietly amongst themselves, until Lord Grandon rose to speak.

"Your Majesty," he said to Aunt Gillian, "Do you wish to reply?"

"Yes, Lord Grandon," she answered resolutely. "The accusations and challenges made by Knor of Shadowray are not only ludicrous, but completely unfounded. The successor is the son of my only sister and is bound by blood and ancient law to be the next in line to the throne. The attempted defamation of the successor's character is slanderous, and completely misinformed. The successor has shown strength of character far beyond his years, coping with the loss of a parent, dealing with the grief of his father, and all the while continuing and excelling in his education. He has come here today with dignity and respect, and has accepted the duties and responsibilities of his position willingly, at great sacrifice to the ways of his previous life. This challenge is nothing more than a futile attempt to defame the reputation of a future monarch, and uselessly stall the legal and natural progression of monarchical order. There is no need to instigate the Rites of Passage until he is of the appropriate and traditional age."

"But by then it will be too late, won't it?" said Knor, darkly.

"You are speaking out of turn, Knor," said Lord Grandon, sternly. "But your Majesty," he continued, addressing Aunt Gillian, "Is it true? Has the successor been accused of attacking his relatives?"

"He has been wrongly accused, by people who misread and contorted his intentions. These alleged attacks were purely circumstantial and blown out of any kind of realistic proportion," she said confidently.

"I see," said Lord Grandon, a hint of doubt in his voice. "Forgive me, your Majesty, but if you have so much faith in the successor, why not let him prove himself beyond any doubt in the Rites of Passage?"

The entire room was buzzing, and Peter noticed a sly grin growing under Knor's shadowed black hood.

"He is far too young, Lord Grandon," said Aunt Gillian reasonably. "The Rites of Passage are taken when one is twice his age. In any case, the heir to the throne should not have to prove his birthright."

Lord Grandon thought for a moment, and then spoke. "Your Majesty," he said, "Again, forgive me, but the successor's bloodline is not what is in question. He has legitimate right to inherit the throne. What is of concern is the readiness to divulge the highest secrets of Galadria to someone who might not be ready, as of now, to receive them. The Rites of Passage would clarify the successor undoubtedly, and following their completion, he would sign the Lorna to the security of us all. True, he is of a young age, but the rites may be modified to be justly suitable. The question then becomes, not why should he accept the Rites of Passage, but why shouldn't he? And thereby clear himself of this rather untraditional introduction to the court."

This was not going at all as expected. Knor was gloating under his hood, and everyone in the room was whispering, and nodding their heads in agreement.

"Lord Grandon," Aunt Gillian started, "Your council is both wise and thoughtful, as always. However, the acceptance or denial of this newfound suggestion does not fall on me. Just as the successor has bravely and dutifully accepted his birthright, so too does the decision fall on him of whether or not to accept this challenge. I request a brief recess to confer with him on this matter."

"Of course, your Majesty," said Lord Grandon, with a small bow.

Aunt Gillian rose, glancing briefly at Peter, who followed. Everyone in the council room stood and bowed to them as they moved to the left side of her throne. The armored guard with the scarlet cloak bowed, then slid open a hidden section of the wall behind him. Entering, Peter noticed the cloaked guard resume his position outside, as the wall slid shut behind him. They were in a small chamber with another golden throne set against the wall, polished benches and tables facing it. Aunt Gillian sat down on one of the benches, ignoring the throne. Peter sat down beside her.

"How bad is this?" he asked, finally able to speak, "What are the Rites of Passage? I remember you mentioning them to me."

"I wasn't counting on this," she said carefully. "The Rites of Passage are a series of four challenges made by the council. They involve surpassing some kind of obstacle to reach each of the four scepters of virtue. Every successor has to go through the rites, but never at such a young age."

Peter was starting to feel dizzy again. He was just expecting to sign his name on the Lorna.

"Are they dangerous?" he asked.

"No. At least not seriously so, and they said they would adjust them to suit your age. Every few weeks you'd attempt one challenge the council has prepared. The thing is, the challenges are never the same, so we wouldn't know what to expect. However, the council and I watch your every move during the challenges. Once the successor finds the scepter, is in mortal danger, or completely gives up, the challenge is over. The successor is also allowed to use their Protava, or sacred weapon. It's a tool they choose and carry with them the rest of their life."

"You went through the Rites of Passage. Do you think I could do them?"

She thought seriously for a moment.

"Yes, I'm sure you could. I trust the council; they'll make the adjustments fair. It's Knor I don't trust."

"What do you think he's up to?" he asked. "The councilman said that I'm assured the throne, and that after the rites I would sign the Lorna. If the council is fair, and is watching me throughout each challenge, how could Knor stop me? You said he couldn't enter Hillside, right?"

"Yes, there's no known way to break into the manor...but I must be honest with you. Knor is very dangerous and very capable. I'm just not sure exactly what he's trying to do, other than stall for time. As the person who initiated the challenge, Knor would be with us in the council room while the rites were happening."

"Maybe he's just hoping I don't pass the challenges," Peter offered.

Aunt Gillian paused for a moment.

"No Willowbrook has ever failed the Rites of Passage. If something were to happen to you during one of the challenges...no one would blame the council for any wrongdoing, and no one could blame Knor since the council prepared the challenges themselves. He could say I forced you to accept a challenge you weren't ready for just to stay in power. It would give him a position to attack me from, to take my place."

Peter felt a knot growing in the pit of his stomach. And he was suddenly starving. He deeply regretted eating all his chocolate bars the night before. Things seemed to be getting worse by the second. Then he remembered the Twickeypoo's chocolates! Reaching into his leather book bag, he thought it was high time for some comfort food.

"But how could he do anything to me?" he asked, as he opened the small, polished wooden chocolate box. "The council prepares the challenges, he's with you in the room, and everyone is watch ..."

"PETER! DON'T EAT THAT!"

"WHAAAT?!!" he yelled in surprise.

Aunt Gillian took the chocolate he was about to put in his mouth and inspected it. Smiling, she took the polished box from him, put the chocolate back in its place, and looked closely at the entire dozen of them.

"You can have some if you want," he said. "It's just that when I have a lot on my mind, I tend to...well, I like chocolate and the Twickeypoos gave me..."

"Mom and dad, of course!" she laughed.

"Huh...you know the Twickeypoos?"

"Peter, Henry and Martha, the Twickeypoos, are your grandparents! We couldn't just let you be raised alone. They're from Galadria!"

"Huh?" he said, dumbstruck. "My what? I didn't think mom's parents...your parents, were still alive...oh wow..."

"They've looked after you to make sure you were taken care of. Since your father and I don't speak frequently they've been the ones telling me how you've been. I didn't know when would be the right time to tell you. They love you very much. And these aren't chocolates, they're Creamers!"

"...wow..."

"They're Creamers, Peter!"

"That's the name of their store," he said, amazed he now had grandparents. "What are Creamers?"

"Things, objects that are made in Galadria act differently here. After a while, certain Galadrian merchants started fine tuning objects for specific results. Creamers are very rare; they must have had them for a long time. When eaten, they give a person very special abilities."

"Like what?" he asked, going along with all of this quite easily.

Then it hit him, where on Earth could Galadria possibly be? After all that's happened, nothing was impossible to him anymore.

"Well, it depends," said Aunt Gillian brightly. "But you can only eat one at a time or they cancel each other out; each one usually only lasts about an hour. Mom and dad know what's been happening here, they probably gave these to you for extra protection."

Still trying to get over Aunt Gillian calling the Twickeypoos 'mom and dad', Peter did remember Mrs. Twickeypoo mentioning something about saving them for special occasions. He trusted the Twickeypoos completely and anything they'd give him would have to help.

"Can I use those during the rites?"

"We'll make the council agree to it," said Aunt Gillian resolutely, a new glimmer of hope in her eyes. "That is, if you want to do this. We could refuse and ..."

"I want to do this," he said. "I already agreed to the role, how could I back down from the first challenge it presents me?"

Aunt Gillian was positively swelling with pride.

"Besides," he added, "If no Willowbrook ever failed them, and I have those, uh, Creamers, I'll be okay."

"And I'll be watching, and so will the council," she said confidently. "If I feel you are in any danger unreasonable for the rites, I'll inform the council and we'll stop the challenge immediately."

As she handed him back his box of Creamers, Peter curiously looked at them and all their different designs. He wondered what each one did.

"How will I know which one to choose? The Twickeypoos didn't tell me what they do."

"Would you have believed them if they did?"

"Well, maybe," But he knew he would never have believed any of this before now. He also remembered his father standing right behind him when the Twickeypoos gave him the Creamers.

A short time later, he and his aunt were out of the small room and back in their respective thrones in front of the court. Peter was holding his box of Creamers firmly in his hands. Lord Grandon was standing.

"Esteemed council," started Aunt Gillian loudly. "The successor has gallantly accepted to undergo the Rites of Passage."

The court burst into applause, and Knor seemed delighted.

"However," she continued, "He does have something to ask of the council."

Everyone in the room leaned forward in their seats.

"The successor's grandparents, his appointed Royal Guardians, gave him a very special gift, one that the successor was not even fully aware of until now. Considering his age, and the short preparation time he will have for the rites, I am sure the council will be fair and wise, and agree with me in letting him use this gift during the challenges."

The entire court was buzzing again. Knor looked livid. This was a twist he did not count on. Even the council looked eager for more information.

"Your Majesty," said Lord Grandon, "Please do tell us, what is this gift?"

"Creamers," said Aunt Gillian triumphantly, looking at Knor. "A box of a dozen assorted Creamers."

The buzzing of the court grew even louder, several people applauded.

Aunt Gillian nodded to Peter, who handed Lord Grandon the Creamers box. Lord Grandon inspected it, gave the slightest hint of a smile, and handed it to the rest of his council mates.

"This is an outrage!" exclaimed Knor. "Why should he have that bonus?"

"I just explained why," said Aunt Gillian quickly. "Weren't you paying attention?"

"Yes," he growled, "Because of his age and his lack of time to prepare for the rites."

"So you agree,"

"No, I don't..."

"But you just said,"

"No, I didn't, I was..."

"You didn't just say that?"

"Yes, but ..."

"But what?"

"What I said was ..."

"My, my, Knor, such indecision. And to think, you want to be next in line to the throne."

The court started echoing with laughter. Peter got the distinct impression no one really liked Knor very much.

"I didn't know what I was saying," Knor said severely.

"That, Knor," said Aunt Gillian cheerily, "is the understatement of the century."

This time, Peter was sure everyone was laughing. Even some of the council members were giggling.

"Silence, please," said Lord Grandon. The court's laughter slowly died down.

"The council has agreed to let the successor use his Creamers as he sees fit."

"But Lord Grandon," injected Knor. "We do not know for certain what abilities the Creamers will give him."

"Neither does he," said Aunt Gillian.

"Then let that stand," said Knor cunningly. "The successor can have no contact with his Royal Guardians until all the rites are completed, and cannot come in contact with anyone who might identify the use of his Creamers. After all," he added, "The rites are meant to challenge the successor. We are not helping him by making it too easy a task for him to complete."

"Your Majesty?" asked Lord Grandon.

Aunt Gillian glanced quickly at Peter, who gave her a small nod. Nothing in that box could be anything but helpful coming from the Twickeypoos.

"The successor agrees," she proclaimed.

Lord Grandon handed Peter the polished wooden box, which he gratefully put back into his leather book bag. Knor was glaring at him coldly.

"And now," continued Lord Grandon, "We come to the subject of the Protava, the successor's sacred weapon. He may choose from an assortment."

Peter didn't know what to do. In the flurry about the Creamers, he had forgotten to ask Aunt Gillian about which weapon to choose for the rites. But before Lord Grandon could speak any further ...

"That will not be necessary," said Aunt Gillian. "The successor already has his Protava. Peter, if you could show the court your boomerang."

He was confused, his boomerang was his sacred weapon? But then he remembered who had given it to him all those years ago,

Mr. Twickeypoo! He pulled his boomerang from his pocket and held it in front of him with both hands.

"Would the successor be willing to show us a small demonstration of his skill?" asked Lord Grandon.

"Peter?" asked Aunt Gillian, looking at him supportively.

He nodded agreeably.

"The successor would be only too happy to accommodate us," she said proudly.

Peter pulled back his arm and threw his boomerang straight at the high domed ceiling directly above the court. It soared swiftly into the air, turned, and was just as quickly back in his hand. The court, including Aunt Gillian, looked on in delight and applauded enthusiastically.

Then, with a twinkle in his eye, Peter threw his boomerang again, this time at Knor. It turned a few feet away from his hooded face...but Knor suddenly stepped forward and caught it.

The applause died down as an uncomfortable silence swept through the room. Peter was shocked, he never meant for his boomerang to make contact with him. Knor coldly inspected the boomerang, then without warning, hurled it back at Peter's face. Peter was barely able to catch it with both hands. He was startled at the strength behind Knor's throw. A few audible gasps were heard from the court.

"I would advise the successor to be more respectful." said Knor sharply. "Like his attacks on his aunt and neighbor, his actions might be... what was the word her Majesty quickly thought up...ah yes, misread."

"I would advise you to be more careful, Knor," said Aunt Gillian protectively. She looked utterly enraged. "Lest the court misread your intentions."

"The court can think whatever it likes, your Majesty, unlike you, my actions have never been dictated by their approval."

"Only by your own twisted ambition," said Aunt Gillian sharply.

"Perhaps, but at least my ambition has never led me to need to hide behind a child for protection."

"Enough Knor!" said Lord Grandon forcefully. "Another word and you shall be escorted from the court. Your Majesty, our apologies," he said, turning to Aunt Gillian.

But she wasn't listening. Her eyes were locked with Knor's, as the two of them defiantly stared each other down.

"Do not try my patience, Knor," she said warningly.

"Your infinite patience? Never, your majesty," he said sarcastically, with a mock bow.

Peter sat there with the rest of the court, watching this battle of formidable wills. Everyone knew how powerful and capable Aunt Gillian was. It was only her inherent sense of decency that was stopping her from dealing with Knor severely. Yet, one thing was blindingly clear, Knor was not afraid of her.

As Peter held his boomerang in his hands, Knor slowly broke his gaze with Aunt Gillian and looked straight at him. A cold wave crept over him as he peered back at Knor's cruel, calculating face. He couldn't help thinking about what lay before him in the months ahead, and what poison this cloaked man had in store for him. As Peter stared back into those empty, metallic eyes, he realized for the first time...he was in very real danger.

6

STUDY, STUDY, STUDY

The next few days were a whirlwind. The Supreme Council decided that the first rite would take place in two weeks, and that the following rites would also be held at two-week intervals. Aunt Gillian worked endless hours with the council, making sure the four challenges were adequately adjusted, and that Knor did not interfere with them in any way. Peter wanted to find out as much as he could about Galadria and had started the rigorous new schedule that Mrs. Smith and Monty had arranged for him.

Monty informed Peter he would be starting tutored sessions in three subjects: Galadrian political science, Galadrian culture, and a special series of sessions to help him use his Protava to its maximum potential. Peter was relieved to hear he would only be studying from two books for his classes. He was quite surprised however, when Monty appeared with these two books and unloaded them on the sturdy oak desk in his room. They were the most massive books Peter had ever seen, larger than phone books and about a foot thick, each tightly bound in dark brown leather. Monty evidently had a struggle carrying them, and broke into a desperate run to drop them on the enormous desk.

Monty also gave Peter two exquisite leather-bound notebooks, and a very interesting and beautiful golden pen, which he said was made in Galadria. He told Peter that when the pen was used here, it never ran out of ink or wrote a misspelled word. Trying it out, Peter opened one of his notebooks and tried to write 'D-A-G' with the intention of spelling 'DOG,' but no matter how many times he tried, the word was always spelled correctly.

Very impressed, he asked Monty why Galadrian-made objects behaved this way. Monty said he had no idea, and that no Galadrian had ever come up with a solid reason, but that since the effects of using some of the objects here were extraordinary, many Galadrian merchants started making them for the sole purpose of using them outside Galadria. Monty noted that in Galadria, Peter's golden pen didn't even write, and fell apart rather easily. But here, it was a prized possession. He went on by saying that not all objects had special powers here, only some, and that a few objects from here behaved very differently in Galadria. Playing cards from here, for instance, would always play themselves and never let anyone else join in. Finally, Peter had to ask where exactly Galadria was and why Monty kept referring to where they were as "here."

"Well, sir," started Monty. "Galadria is 'here,' meaning on Earth, but is in a different dimension that can only be reached through portals."

"Portals?" asked Peter, looking up from his large oak desk as he flipped through his thick book on Galadrian culture. Printed in gold, on the leather cover, was the title, *Golden Civilizations: The Story of Galadria*.

"Yes, sir," continued Monty, "They look like pools of light. You just step into them, and you're instantly back in Galadria, or wherever else the portal is built to go to. Our portal here at Hillside is in the council room."

"Oh...so that's how the Galadrian court just shows up out of nowhere. But what's to keep people from using portals to break into places, like here at Hillside?"

"Attack trained squirrels."

"What?"

"Nothing, sir," said Monty, chuckling. "Portals are strictly controlled by the Supreme Council, and are built and registered to go only to specific, designated areas. For instance, the portal in our council room only leads to its corresponding portal in The Great Palace in Galadria, and nowhere else. Also, portals can be switched off at either end. If we switched off the one in the council room, for instance, no one from The Great Palace would be able to travel through, even if the portal on their side is open. Most of the portals in Galadria are owned by the ruling noble families, and usually only take them back and forth from their homes in other realms."

"Is there another Willowbrook home?" asked Peter.

"This is the official Willowbrook residence, though there is another one in Galadria."

"Aunt Gillian must be in Galadria a lot, huh?"

"Mistress Gillian is always traveling by portal," said Monty, checking his watch. "But since portal travel is quite instantaneous, it never impedes one's time. Now, I think I should let you get some rest. First thing in the morning, after breakfast, you shall start your new lessons."

Peter spent the rest of the night flipping through the endless pages of his books. His political science book, *The Noble Families of Galadria,* was extensive and very interesting. Searching for the Willowbrook family, he flipped through page after page of long histories, intricate ancestries and pleasant family portraits, until he read the heading, '*Chapter 65: The Noble House of Shadowray.*' None of the members of Shadowray were smiling in the slightest. Not even an ironic grin was to be found. They all wore black shrouds, from the scowling grandparents to the screaming infants. The least severe of them had white lining breaking up their dark attire, but that was all. Some of their faces were not even visible, being completely shadowed by their hoods. Despite this, he noticed their family was very accomplished, having major leaders in science and business. They were also one of the wealthiest clans and had a very old bloodline. Peter scoured the pictures for Knor, but only found a single, cold portrait of him, stiffly seated on a large, elaborate, twisted, steel chair. The caption under his photograph was impressive.

Knor Shadowray, seated on the ancestral Shadowray chair, once owned by his great grandfather, the Honorable Councilman, Putrus Shadowray. Knor, third in line to the Galadrian throne, has an Elwin Mastery in Political Science and Economics, is a founding member of the Knights of Metallin, and is a four time recipient of the Order of the Condra, for outstanding achievement in dimensional commerce.

Photo courtesy of The Noble House of Shadowray Archives, Galadria.

"Third in line to the throne?" Peter thought to himself, "Who's...oh, mom. She was first in line, and Knor's third...but...that means...I'm in this book!"

About an hour later, he found what he was looking for. *'Chapter 104: The Noble House of Willowbrook.'* Like the rest of the royal families, except for the Shadowrays, the Willowbrook families all looked positively cheerful. Almost everyone had different variations of thick, brown hair. The Willowbrooks were also among the wealthiest clans, and had leaders in politics, business and the arts. They had a long list of Galadrian rulers, and Peter instantly spotted a beautiful portrait of Aunt Gillian, seated on her golden throne. The caption under it read:

Her Royal Majesty, Queen Gillian of the Noble House of Willowbrook, Supreme Ruler of the Realm of Galadria. Before Queen Gillian's coronation, she was already a hard working, accomplished crown princess, having achieved an Elwin Mastery in Dimensional Diplomacy and Political Science, was a Founding Princess of the Mists of the Three Lakes, was the second Galadrian princess to ever become a Knight of the Leaf, and was four time recipient of the Order of Lindiwim, for outstanding achievement in dimensional intermediary diplomacy. As Queen...

It went on forever. Peter was very proud, and very intimidated. Searching carefully, he meticulously scanned every picture he saw. Moments later, he found it. It was a lovely portrait of his mother, sitting on a chair in a garden, wearing an elegant blue gown. Peter just stared at her kind face. She looked so content. Slowly, he read the caption below it.

Princess Patricia Willowbrook, next in line to the Galadrian throne, sitting in one of the many beautiful gardens at the Willowbrook Earth Estate, Hillside Manor. Princess Patricia has recently just had her first baby boy, Peter. The famously private princess lives most of her life on

Earth, and has declined, as of yet, to provide a photo of the new baby prince. She does, however, show the deepest gratitude for the support and joy shown by the Galadrian people at the birth of her new son. Princess Patricia is a Princess of the Mists of the Three Lakes, and has been a recipient of the Order of Vinelle, for outstanding achievement in bettering the lives of the less fortunate.

Photo courtesy of the Noble House of Willowbrook Archives, Galadria.

Peter was shocked to see his own name, and filled with the deepest sense of pride for his mother. He had no idea what the 'Three Lakes' thing was, but he never knew she was honored for anything, much less for helping the less fortunate. But more questions plagued him. Why wasn't his father mentioned? Why did his mother decide to live privately away from all this? The only reason Peter could think of was that she wanted to protect him from ambitious personalities like Knor and his family. After what he'd seen and read about Knor and the Shadowrays, he decided that that was a really good reason. Yet, here he was, being challenged by Knor...at any rate, this book was obviously not recent, and he had a lot more pressing matters to focus on. Glancing down the page, another photograph grabbed his attention. It was a small one, of two young girls wearing little beribboned dresses, one blue, and the other, light gold. Both girls had hair the color of caramel, and were laughing happily. The girl in the blue dress was holding a yawning, white tiger cub. Neither girl could have been older than ten. The caption under the picture read:

Crown Princess Gillian Willowbrook looks on, as her younger sister, Princess Patricia, lovingly holds their new Galadrian white tiger cub, Rune, in one of the many gardens of the sprawling Willowbrook Earth Estate, Hillside Manor.

Photo courtesy of the Noble House of Willowbrook Archives, Galadria.

Peter had never seen any childhood photographs of his mother. He was exceedingly happy to be looking at one. Marking the page, he continued to search for more. The Willowbrook chapter, however, revealed itself to be abundantly thick. Hours later, he drowsily leaned his head on his book, promising himself he would only rest his eyes for a few minutes.

"Sir...Sir..." said Monty. "Oh no, I hope you haven't slept like that all night."

Peter reluctantly opened his eyes, revealing the enlarged, blurred letters of the book in front of him. It was morning; he had fallen asleep on his desk, his forehead and nose squashed uncomfortably against the sheer bulk of his political science book. Pushing himself up with both hands, a page of the book seemed to have permanently attached itself to his forehead. Pulling it off, he painfully raised his head, assisting himself with both hands.

"Owwwwwww," he said, massaging his stiff neck.

"Rough night, sir?" asked Monty, who walked cheerfully toward him with his breakfast tray. "Not to worry, I have just the thing for that... bacon and waffles!"

Monty pushed Peter's books to one side and placed his breakfast tray on the enormous oak desk in front of him. The tray was littered with plates full of long strips of crispy bacon, a cheese omelet, high stacks of golden brown waffles, and next to it, eight little bottles of different colored syrups.

"After breakfast," Monty continued, checking his watch, "We should head straight away to your political science lesson. Mr. Frank is eager to get you started as soon as possible."

"Where is Mr. Frank from?" he asked, pouring what he hoped was maple syrup onto his waffles.

"All your tutors reside here in the manor, sir," said Monty, stacking Peter's books and notebooks on top of each other. "Mr. Frank, your political science tutor, oversees the manor Library. Ms. Homebody, your Galadrian culture tutor, helps Madam Cornhen run the manor's history museum, and Mr. Harden, your Protava trainer, is in charge of our animal preserve. They are all very well studied in their respective fields."

After finishing breakfast, Peter and Monty set out for his new study room, each carrying a thick, cumbersome book. Monty informed him that his academic lessons would take place in the same room, while Mr. Harden would hold his lessons in the gardens. After a quiet walk down the halls, they entered a barren, high ceilinged room, with high arched windows and a door leading outside. In the middle of the empty room, directly facing each other, were two sets of wooden desks and chairs. A very elderly man with gray hair, wearing a tweed suit and thick glasses, was standing behind the larger desk. The same massive political science book Peter had was in front of him. After putting down their books on the smaller desk, Monty made the introduction.

"Sir," Monty said formally, "May I present Mr. Barry Frank. Mr. Frank will be acting as your political science tutor this summer."

"Hello Mr. Frank," said Peter, offering to shake his hand.

"HELLO MASTER HUDDLESTON," said Mr. Frank, in a loud, stern voice, shaking Peter's hand stiffly.

"Well," said Monty cheerfully, "If anyone needs me, I shall be standing by the door."

"YOU'LL BE FIGHTING A BOAR?" asked Mr. Frank, yelling.

"What? No, sir," continued Monty, in a considerably louder voice, "I'll be standing next to the DOOR."

"All right then!" Mr. Frank replied.

Mr. Frank, the librarian, was turning out to be rather deaf. As they both took their respective seats in front of their desks, Peter got out his Galadrian golden pen from his leather book bag.

"Now, look here Master Huddleston," said Mr. Frank strictly. "I run a tight ship and have made a very simple study plan for our lessons. Here it is. Are you ready? Here we go.

"Everyday, you're going to read as much as you can of that entire book, and take detailed notes. If you have any questions, ask me, and at the end of each chapter, you'll take a test to make sure you understood it all. This is a very important subject and we're going to read every inch of that book, cover to cover."

"The entire book?" Peter asked, glancing at the enormous volume in front of him."

"Twice," said Mr. Frank, grinning.

"Twice!"

"Twice. Now, let's begin. We've already wasted three minutes. Notebook and pen out, page one start reading."

Peter opened the intimidating book to its first page and began to read the tiny writing.

"OUT LOUD, Master Huddleston," shouted Mr. Frank, startling Peter. "I'll be following you from my own book, I want to make sure you're getting every word of this."

"The ruling families of..."

"WHAT? WHAT DID YOU SAY?"

"THE RULING FAMILIES OF..."

Peter spent the next few hours reading to Mr. Frank and taking notes in this same manner. By the time his lesson was over, his throat was extremely sore.

"TIME'S UP, Master Huddleston," said Mr. Frank, standing, struggling to pick up his own book. "I'll expect you to have gone over your notes before tomorrow."

As Mr. Frank slowly shuffled out of the room, Peter stood up and stretched his tired back. He had barely taken a breath, when...

"Gooood moooorning!" sang an extremely cheerful voice.

Peter turned to see a plump, exceptionally jolly looking woman standing next to Monty at the doorway. She was wearing a light pink dress with a large, matching rimmed round hat that was perched neatly on top of her white-blond hair. She was carrying the same thick cultural studies book that was on his desk.

"Oh, I didn't see you there, Montgomery, don't you look dapper today," she said jollily, making Monty's face go red.

"Ms. Homebody, may I introduce ..."

"Montgomery, please," she continued, cheerily waving her hand. "You know I won't say a word to you unless you call me Jessica."

"But Ms. Home..."

"Jessica."

"But it's not prop..."

"JE-SSI-CA,"

"But..."

"Say it with me, JE-SSI-CA,"

"Oh, alright! Jessica," said Monty exasperatedly, "May I introduce you to Master Huddleston. Sir, this is Ms. Homebody."

Peter had barely taken a step forward to shake her hand, when she rushed towards him, threw her book on her desk, and gave him a very strong hug.

"Master Huddleston!" she swooned with delight. "I'm so glad we're going to be working together! When I told my mother, I said, 'Mother, guess who I'll be teaching? Guess! You'll never guess! Master Peter Huddleston! Ahhhhhhh!' She almost fainted right then and there, I swear she almost did!"

Ms. Homebody swiftly sat behind her desk and gave Peter a huge smile. Winded by her hug, he slowly took his seat as well.

"Now, I've been thinking about this lesson and here's what I thought. Are you ready?"

Peter thought Ms. Homebody was about to burst from sheer excitement. She was an absolute ball of energy.

"I've decided," she continued, "To have you read every page of this book out loud and make notes of it in your notebook! And every now and then, we'll have...oh, I wouldn't call them tests, we'll have little written exercises to make sure you've understood everything! What do you think? Don't you just love it? I love it!"

"Um...sure," he replied, trying not to sound too deflated. "Sounds good."

"Doesn't it!" she happily screamed. "I knew you'd love it! Alright now, let's begin, page one."

Peter flipped open his Galadrian culture book and started reading aloud, every now and then writing notes in his notebook. Every time he glanced over at Ms. Homebody, she was beaming at him with a blinding smile on her face. Hours later, as he was reading about how chocolate was the most popular Galadrian food, Ms. Homebody suddenly shut her book and jumped out of her chair.

"Alright, that's it!" she said cheerfully, holding her book in her arms. "You did wonderfully, Master Huddleston! Wonderfully! Your voice, it's so soothing. Just review your notes and I'll see you tomorrow! Taaa Taaa!"

Ms. Homebody zoomed towards the door, next to Monty.

"See you tomorrow, Montgomery," she said breathlessly, leaving Monty blushing by the door.

"She's really chipper, isn't she?" Peter asked, rubbing his tired eyes.

"Who? Oh, Ms. Homebody?" Monty asked, as if he didn't know whom Peter was talking about. "She does have a rather happy disposition, doesn't she? Yes...lovely woman."

"Uh huh," said Peter, smiling.

"What, sir?"

"Oh...nothing," Peter continued. "She seems to like you."

"What-no-who? Ms. Homebody?"

"Yeah, you know, JE-SSI-CA,"

"Well...huh...I...um...look, it's time for lunch," he said, suddenly looking at his watch. "Here sir, let me help you with those books."

They dropped off the heavy volumes in Peter's room and headed hungrily for the dining hall. After a lunch of lamb pie, and a creamy chocolate pudding for dessert, they were back in the barren study room waiting for Peter's next tutor, Mr. Harden.

"Now where could he be?" asked Monty concernedly.

Just then, the door to the gardens burst open to reveal a tall, burly figure standing at the doorway.

"Good afternoon, Master Huddleston," said the man in a rough, yet friendly voice. "Hey there Monty, good to see you."

"Hi," said Peter, distracted by the man's attire. He was wearing what looked like a flexible type of dark brown leather armor, thick gloves with the fingers cut out, and sturdy leather boots. He had short blond hair and his face was very sun burnt.

"Name's Ben Harden, Master Huddleston," he said, walking up to Peter and shaking his hand heftily. "But please call me Ben."

"Nice to meet you Ben, you can call me Peter, if you want,"

"I'll do that then. Well, I hear you've got quite a unique Protava there, Peter."

"Oh, yeah," he said, pulling his boomerang out of his pocket and handing it to Ben.

"I'll be..." said Ben curiously, taking Peter's boomerang and looking at it closely. "How long have you had it?"

"A couple of years,"

"Use it a lot?" asked Ben, weighing the boomerang in his hands.

"Pretty much all the time," Peter replied, wondering what Ben was doing. He was tapping the boomerang forcefully against the hard floor.

"I'm certain your boomerang's Galadrian made," said Ben confidently.

"Really? Oh yeah, I guess it would be. It was given to me by Mr. Twickey...uh, by my grandfather."

"Have you noticed anything unusual about it?"

"Not really," he said, trying to remember anything out of the ordinary. "It flies pretty well...it's fast. But nothing really unusual."

"Well, I've noticed something," said Ben, holding the boomerang so closely to his eyes that it was touching his nose. "There isn't a scratch on it, not even the tiniest mark. And for someone who's had it for years and uses it all the time, that's quite a feat. We're in luck, Peter. Your Protava probably has special abilities, seeing as how it's Galadrian made. C'mon, show me what it can do."

Ben led Peter out of the barren study room, onto the flat, grassy lawns and high walled bushes of the garden outside. Monty followed quickly behind them. The warm sun and cool breeze felt fantastic after being indoors reading and taking notes all day.

They walked to the middle of the lawn when Ben handed Peter back his boomerang and gestured for him to use it. Peter pulled back his arm and threw his boomerang high up into the air. It turned quickly and zoomed back to them, landing lightly in his hand.

"Blimey," said Ben excitedly. "You're good with that thing, aren't you? And fast! Wasn't it, Monty?"

"Yes, sir," said Monty, standing happily in the shade of the manor. "Very impressive."

"We'll probably be moving even faster than I'd hoped," Ben continued enthusiastically.

"Great," said Peter, "But Ben, what exactly is a Protava? I mean, what's it really for?"

"Well, a Protava is the sacred weapon of any ruler or successor to the throne of Galadria. Many ruling nobles have them as well. They usually carry it with them most of their lives. Not only is it used during the Rites of Passage, but it's also a visual symbol of strength. Protavas are extremely rare because of the combination of materials needed to endow them with special powers."

"But does that mean they don't have any special abilities when you're in Galadria?"

"No, they do," Ben replied. "That's why Protavas are so rare. They contain specific properties and elements from both Galadria and Earth, so they work just as well in both places. It takes a long time to build a proper Protava."

"You said all Galadrian rulers have one, but Aunt Gillian isn't carrying a Protava."

"Sure she is," said Ben, a little surprised. "Mistress Gillian's Protava is a very powerful one at that, a leeana. It's that golden rope she has hanging at her side."

"That's a Protava?" asked Peter. "A leeana?"

"Sure is," said Ben. "And I heard she's a master at it, too. Tricky things leeanas, but once you get the hang of them, they're very effective."

"How?"

"A leeana's strength is directly proportionate to the person wielding it. When not in use, it's like a smooth, strong length of rope, but when wielded, can become as hard as any metal and completely unbreakable. When used by a master, as with Mistress Gillian, a leeana can be commanded into action, even when its wielder is not in physical contact with it, although I've heard that takes a lot of concentration."

"What does mine do?" asked Peter excitedly.

"Well...to tell you the truth, I'm not sure. I've never heard of a boomerang being a Protava. I've heard of Protava swords, wompos, shields, glees, whips..."

"Uh-huh," said Peter, not sure whether or not he should be concerned about this. "What's a wompo?"

"A wompo is basically one, or a pair of gloves. When used correctly, they greatly enhance the strength of the wearer. Being near indestructible, they're excellent for climbing."

"And glees?"

"I've never actually seen a glee, but I read that a princess of ancient Galadria used one. It was a lady's evening fan. Once, a rival political family tried to have her kidnapped and she was able to knock out all six of her adversaries. She opened her fan and rhythmically wielded it, creating a high-pitched whistle. When she whipped the fan in their direction, the sound was so intense and deafening, it assaulted and overloaded their senses. Glees use sound as a weapon."

"Wow, that's pretty cool. I wonder if my boomerang has hidden powers?"

"By the looks of it," continued Ben, "I'd say your boomerang can't break, or even be damaged. It's also unusually fast and seems to be able to travel exceptionally far distances before returning. What I'd like to concentrate on, at least for today, is for you to show me the limits of your control over it. Throw it as far as you can, as hard as you can, and as lightly as you can. I'd also like to see how precisely you can control its direction, and your aim with it. After we've seen all that, we'll take it from there."

The rest of the day, Peter threw his boomerang every which way he could think of. After his first lesson, both he and Ben were pleased with the results, though Peter's arm was very, very sore.

The next few days followed this same schedule and eventually Peter began to get used to it. His long hours of study with Mr. Frank and Ms. Homebody were well balanced by his physical Protava training with Ben. He was enjoying all three lessons thoroughly. In Ms. Homebody's class, he learned, among other things, that each of the four Rites of Passage was made to test each of the four traits valued by Galadrian society. The four stars on the Galadrian crest were symbols of these traits, being perseverance, cleverness, virtue and courage.

Peter also learned that the sole objective during each Rite of Passage was to overcome whatever obstacle was presented, and acquire the Galadrian Golden Scepters that would await him at the end of each challenge.

Reading aloud to Ms. Homebody, Peter was surprised to find out that despite its reputation as the Golden Realm, Galadria itself produced very little gold. In fact, any amount of Galadrian gold was extremely rare. Usually only the highest-ranking nobles would own Galadrian gold objects. This made him appreciate the golden Galadrian pen he was holding even more. As he continued reading, he discovered that the most predominant metal in Galadria was an almost transparent, crystal-like substance known as Galamere, and that most of the architecture in Galadria was made from it.

At his Protava lessons, Ben was trying to get him to wield his boomerang like a throwing knife. Now that they were certain it could not be damaged, Peter repetitively threw it into a wooden plank, intending to make it stick to the board like a hurled knife would, then, through sheer will, command it to return to his hand. Although it took Peter awhile to readjust to the idea of hurling, rather than just throwing his boomerang, it was soon deeply embedded into the thick wooden plank. It was commanding it to come back that was tricky.

"Come on...come on back..." said Peter, intensely staring, wide eyed, at his embedded boomerang. "Come...back...now...dammit..."

"Umm...good effort," said Ben supportively, "But remember, with Protavas it's not so much telling them what to do that works, it's more thinking, envisioning them doing what you want, with complete clarity, confidence and certainty. It takes a while to learn. You have to get over the logical part of your brain telling you that there's no reason an object should respond to your thoughts. You have to get out of your own way. This is an excellent exercise to bond you with your boomerang and teach you how to start mentally controlling it. Try again..."

After a long day of lessons, Peter would usually have an early dinner and head back to his room, discussing what he had learned that day with Monty. At night, nestled in his comfy bed, he would reach into his book bag and open his polished wooden box of chocolate Creamers. He had gotten into the habit of curiously studying them and wondering what new ability each of them would give him. He was sure the different designs and colors on each Creamer were a clue, but they still weren't specifically spelled out and the possibilities seemed endless.

One Creamer was light blue, imprinted with a golden wing, which he excitedly hoped would make him fly. But the other Creamers weren't so easy to interpret. One was dark blue with a little red fish on it. Next to that was a green one shaped like a clover, then a purple one with a howling wolf on it. There was a gray one with a spider, a round, plump milk chocolate with a red cross, one with a clenched fist, one with a hummingbird, one that looked like a marshmallow, one that was different shades of blue with stars and a moon, a plump, green leaf shaped one, and in the center of the box, a round, black Creamer with a white skull and crossbones. He did not like the look of this one at all.

As Peter's first rite loomed closer, he began to feel more and more agitated. He wasn't the only one. Monty had gotten into the habit of nonchalantly mentioning random Galadrian facts, everything from how to drink Galadrian hot chocolate, to the giant eagles that occupied the highest Galadrian mountaintops.

Mr. Frank and Ms. Homebody had started constantly drilling Peter on everything he had read, all in a seeming attempt to cram as much information into him before his first challenge. Ben's Protava lessons were also lasting much longer, and would often extend late into the night.

Aunt Gillian was completely confident Peter would perform well. During the few times they were able to have lunch, she would calmly assure him that the council's challenges were appropriate, then would casually inquire about the progress of his lessons. She also wanted to know if he had heard any more strange noises coming from outside his door, but to her relief, nothing unusual had occurred.

Time passed startlingly fast, as it usually does when one doesn't want it to, and Peter found himself sitting in his room on the day of the first rite.

He was relieved that he would be able to wear his own comfortable clothes for the rites. Peter's boomerang was in its familiar spot, protruding from his pants pocket, and his Creamers box was snugly nestled in the brown leather book bag that was strapped securely across his chest.

Feeling rather anxious, he generously partook of the white chocolate truffles piled high on the silver tray on the center table of his room.

Just as Peter popped the last truffle into his mouth, Monty entered the room. Moments later, they were standing in the small hall leading to the council room. Monty and Mrs. Smith were poised and ready to pull open the high arched doors. Peter could hear his own heart pounding furiously in his chest.

"Mistress Gillian is seated on her throne," said Mrs. Smith, managing a nervous sort of smile.

Knowing that the entire Galadrian court was anxiously awaiting his arrival, Peter closed his eyes and tried to calm himself down. He kept reminding himself that no member of the Willowbrook family had ever failed the Rites of Passage. They couldn't possibly be that difficult. Steadying himself, he nodded for Monty and Mrs. Smith to pull open the doors.

7

THROUGH THE LOOKING GLASS

As the doors opened, Peter saw the entire Galadrian court assembled in the domed council room. Aunt Gillian was seated on her throne, surrounded by the same eight guards in golden armor. In front of her was what looked like a very large, round wading pool. The pool appeared to be carved from stone and the water in it was glowing.

The scarlet-cloaked guard standing next to Aunt Gillian stepped forward and raised his hand for the court's attention.

"Ladies and gentlemen of the court," he loudly proclaimed, "It is my great honor to present to you, Peter Willowbrook Huddleston, of the Noble House of Willowbrook, and successor to the Galadrian throne."

The court turned as one to see Peter standing at the doorway. His heart was pounding violently in his chest. He walked slowly down the steps toward Aunt Gillian, desperately hoping not to trip and roll into the glowing wading pool. As he descended, the formally dressed members of the court smiled fondly and bowed their heads. He stood next to Aunt Gillian, giving a slight bow to the council. They all bowed back to him in unison. Knor was standing directly across from the council, coldly observing him from his golden podium.

"Ladies and gentlemen of the court, and esteemed members of the Supreme Council," started Aunt Gillian, "We are here today to witness the successor, Peter Willowbrook Huddleston of the Noble House of Willowbrook, undergo the first of the four traditional Rites of Passage. The rite will be successfully completed when the successor returns with one of the golden scepters. The gold scepters, made here at the Willowbrook Earth Estate, will be placed in the ceremonial holding case by my side."

Peter glanced over and saw a transparent, carved crystal case in front of the armored guards.

"Once all four scepters are in place," Aunt Gillian continued, "The Rites of Passage will be complete. The court and council will watch the rites through the Pollana, the looking glass, which will follow the successor throughout every step of his challenge. Due to added security precautions, the main portal of the council room will not be used to transport the successor. Instead, he will step into the Pollana, which will act as a portal and transport him directly to and from the Algora Realm, where his challenges will take place. And now, we all officially bear witness to the Rites of Passage of Peter Willowbrook Huddleston."

Lord Grandon handed Peter a small, empty, jeweled hourglass.

"When you reach the beginning of the first rite," the councilman said quietly, "The top of the hourglass will fill with sand and will start to time you. You must have the gold scepter in your hand and be in the portal before the top of the hourglass is empty. No movement or change of position will keep the sand from falling. The large stone pool in front of us is called the Pollana.

"Do you understand?"

Peter nodded, looking anxiously at the empty hourglass. Lord Grandon turned to the court.

"The successor will now step into the Pollana for the first rite."

The court fell silent. Peter could feel their excitement. Holding the hourglass in one hand, he walked up to the glowing Pollana and slowly stepped inside. Half expecting to be sucked in by some cosmic force, he was relieved to see that nothing immediate happened. He was standing in some kind of liquid light and felt himself slowly sinking into it, like quicksand. Turning to Aunt Gillian, he saw that she was smiling at him reassuringly. Looking down at the eerie light surrounding him, he felt nothing as he sank deeper and deeper into it. As the light reached his nose, he closed his eyes and prepared for the worst.

There was absolute silence. Opening his eyes, he found he had left the council room. He was still standing in the carved stone Pollana, except now it was empty, devoid of its mysterious glow. Looking up, he was surprised to see a wall full of countless identical golden scepters! The wall was hundreds of feet high and seemed to continue endlessly down both ends of the cavern. Behind him, lighting the dark cave, were several large, ten-foot high, brightly glowing globes. He was trying to figure out what to do, when he glanced at the hourglass in his hand. Its top half was full of smooth, white sand that was quickly emptying into the chasm below it.

Peter stood frozen, staring blankly at the endless wall of golden scepters in front of him. Figuring that the court was somehow watching him now anyway, he began to speak out loud.

"Alright," he said quickly, trying to organize his thoughts, "Each rite is supposed to be about one of the four traits prized by Galadrians... perseverance, cleverness, virtue and courage. This can't be about perseverance, because I only have a small amount of time, or courage, because I don't feel fearful about anything. I don't see how being virtuous could really help me here either. So this must be about cleverness!"

He looked at the hourglass, the top was already one fourth empty.

"Cleverness," he said quickly, pulling his eyes away from the diminishing sand.

"I have to find one specific scepter from an endless wall of them. But...I can't reach past a certain point, and no one knows exactly what the Creamers do, so... so it must be a scepter I can reach."

Peter ran to the wall and tried to pull off as many scepters as he could. They were all vertically embedded into the dense rock and were impossible to move. He reached his arm straight up and jumped. He could only reach until the fifth row of scepters.

"Okay..." he said, thinking frantically. The top of the hourglass was now halfway empty. "It must be one of the scepters below the sixth row, because I can't reach the others to pull them off. But there's no time to check all of them...wait! Aunt Gillian just said that the real scepter was made at Hillside Manor, on Earth, which means...it's made of Earth gold? Well duh. But...they can't all be real gold, there's too many of them. I guess they could just be brass or some other metal. In Galadria, there's hardly any gold at all...only Galamere. These scepters were probably made in Galadria, if they were, they're probably made of Galamere! But...Galamere is nearly transparent, these are golden...most of Galadria's architecture is made of it, but if the cities appear golden, especially during the day, then what makes the transparent Galamere appear golden is... light!"

In moments, Peter's boomerang was flying through the air, effortlessly shattering one of the brightly glowing globes. The cavern became slightly darker. It had worked. The scepters were still golden, but instantly looked somewhat faded. He threw his boomerang again and again, shattering two more glowing globes.

Peter stepped back from the wall and peered at the scepters. They all looked like they had been transformed into crystal. He quickly scanned the first five rows, searching for a scepter that was still golden. He thought his plan had failed...until he found it! The golden scepter was on his far right...on the seventh row. With a running start, he jumped as high as he could, arm outstretched, grasping for the scepter. He still didn't reach it.

Peter glanced at the hourglass. It was less than one fourth full. Holding his boomerang with his outstretched hand, he jumped up and tried to jab the scepter with his Protava's thin edge. Nothing happened. He tried again. And again, he continued leaping and striking at the scepter desperately until he was nearly exhausted. Finally, the scepter popped out of the wall, falling into his arms.

He knew his time was up, and Peter sprinted towards the Pollana, the stone pool already emitting its mysterious glow. Running as fast as he could, he dove headfirst into the light.

Peter's boomerang, hourglass and gold scepter were still nestled tightly in his embrace, as he sprawled huffing and puffing on the Pollana floor. Sitting up, he was startled to see hundreds of faces silently staring at him in intense concentration. All at once, the faces erupted into a bellowing roar of cheers and applause.

"AHHHHHHH!!!" yelled Peter, jolted by the court's enthusiastic response. He felt a light hand on his shoulder and turned to see Aunt Gillian reaching down to him from outside the Pollana, beaming at him with pride. After stuffing his boomerang back in his pocket, he looked at the jeweled hourglass and saw that he only had a few grains of sand left for time.

Stepping out of the Pollana, he handed the jeweled hourglass and gold scepter to Lord Grandon, and then stood next to his aunt. Knor looked absolutely unaffected by his success. He merely stood there, a dark presence in the midst of a joyous crowd. Lord Grandon placed the gold scepter into the carved, crystal ceremonial case where it could be clearly seen. He nodded respectfully to Aunt Gillian.

"Peter Willowbrook Huddleston," said Aunt Gillian loudly, "Has returned bearing the Scepter of Cleverness. He has gallantly completed his first rite in front of us all, and has succeeded without using a single one of his Creamers. I am proud to declare that the first Rite of Passage is complete!"

The court once again broke out in enthusiastic applause. Peter turned and bowed to the council. He felt immensely relieved. Aunt Gillian leaned over and whispered in his ear.

"I'm so proud of you, Peter," she said happily. "You did it!"

✳ ✳ ✳

The next day, Peter resumed his regular schedule of lessons. Despite having successfully completed the first rite, he was very relieved he had another two weeks until his second rite. All three of his tutors were delighted that he completed his first challenge. Even Mr. Frank said he did an "adequate" job. Peter took this as an outpouring of praise. Ms. Homebody, on the other hand, hugged him so hard that he thought he'd dislocated a rib. She also presented him with a congratulatory tin of triple chocolate fudge bars that her mother had made. The fudge turned out to be delicious, though he could hardly keep from laughing when she insisted that Monty try some. She proceeded to make loud airplane noises before popping bits of fudge into his mouth.

"C'mon Montgomery, just one more little bite! Who wants the airplane? Who wants the airplane? NYWEEEEEERRR-NYWEEEEERRR... open up!"

Even though Monty looked like he was about to pass out from embarrassment, Peter noticed that he didn't refuse when Ms. Homebody kept offering him more fudge.

Ben, however, was beside himself with excitement and wanted to know if Peter was able to use any of the techniques they had studied in class. Although Peter had not made much headway with trying to mentally control his boomerang, other than almost going cross eyed from concentration, he was happy to tell Ben how easily the glowing globes had shattered from the strength of his throw.

The excitement of the test eventually tapered off, as Peter found himself reading out loud to Mr. Frank and Ms. Homebody, taking detailed notes in his leather bound notebooks. During one of Ms. Homebody's classes, Madam Cornhen, head of the manor's history museum, stopped by to give him a special briefing on the social customs of the everyday Galadrian. Madam Cornhen was a tall, thin, immaculately groomed woman, who fashioned her silver hair in a tight bun on the back of her head. She wore an elegant, gray dress suit, complimented by a shiny silver belt that was wrapped tightly around her slim waist.

"Master Huddleston, may I introduce Madam Cornhen. She's my boss at the museum!" said Ms. Homebody, excitedly.

"Jessica please, I think of myself as your friend, not your boss." said Madam Cornhen affectionately. "It's an honor to meet you, Master Huddleston."

"Nice to meet you too, Madam Cornhen."

"Congratulations on completing your first rite. It's a great accomplishment. We're all very proud of you."

"Oh, thank you."

"Anyway," she continued, "Today, I was planning to talk to you about..."

"About everyday Galadriaaaaans!" shouted Ms. Homebody, unable to contain her overwhelming enthusiasm. "Sorry to interrupt, Madam Cornhen!"

"Not at all, dear. Just remember what we talked about, when you feel overly excited..."

"I take deep breaths..." said Ms. Homebody, hyperventilating.

"Yes, dear. You mustn't forget to-"

"Breathe! Yes ma'am!" Ms. Homebody cheerfully added. "I love it! It really works! I also continuously think positive thoughts, always; you have to! The other day, I was cooking a pot roast with mother..."

"Jessica..."

"And I told her, 'Mother, you must read this book on positive thinking that Madam Cornhen recommended'...

"Jessica..."

"But you know mother, she said, 'Save your money and take up baking, that's how your father and I have stayed together for forty-one years. I've never met a man who likes cupcakes more than your father.' I said, 'Mother, not everyone likes cupcakes, they're fattening, and...'"

"Jessica!" said Madam Cornhen, a twitch forming at the corner of her eye. "We should get to the lesson plan, now..."

"Lesson plan! Yes! Everyday Galadrians! Go!"

"Now, where was I..." Madam Cornhen continued, regaining her thoughts. "Ah yes, Galadrian life. I thought it best if..."

"Madam Cornhen...your eye is twitching again..." Ms. Homebody noted.

"Yes, dear. It seems to happen when..."

"I call it, 'Mr. Twitchingson.'"

"Yes, I know Jessica, I've asked you not to. It's actually a serious condi..."

"Mr. Twitchingson Vanderplop."

"Okaaaaay..." sighed Madam Cornhen, exhaustedly pressing her fingers against her spasmodic eye.

After Madam Cornhen's eye calmed down, she taught Peter all about the social customs of the everyday Galadrian. Some of the more interesting things he learned were that Galadrian pears were traditionally eaten at farewell dinners, that Galadrian chocolate snow fudge, despite being exceptionally difficult to eat, was a popular gift to bring to parties and celebrations, and that, very simply, Galadrians loved food. Their entire social culture revolved around it.

The Galadrians also emphasized hard work, a core value of its culture. Peter was charmed by the simplicity and practicality of the customs he was learning about.

At night, after his lessons, Peter would leisurely flip through different sections of his books. He tried to find more pictures of his mother in his political science book, but all he found was a tiny image of her in a large group shot. He did, however, find a few more photographs of his aunt when she was younger. One of them was Aunt Gillian at seventeen, vigorously spiraling a golden rope in front of her. The caption under the photograph read:

Crown Princess Gillian Willowbrook at Hillside Manor, the Willowbrook Earth Estate, practicing tirelessly with her chosen Protava, the leeana. The leeana, or Galadrian Rope of Strength, is a symbol of both durability and tenacity. Here, the Crown Princess practices the powerful Spirilla Technique.

Photo courtesy of the Noble House of Willowbrook Archives, Galadria.

Peter laughed out loud when he found another photograph of his younger aunt, messily eating a huge piece of frosted Galadrian chocolate cake with her hands, as a much younger Monty frantically ran after her with a table napkin.

✳ ✳ ✳

Fueled by his success in the first rite, the days passed happily by as Peter continued his education. He learned that although minor feuds existed between some of the ruling nobles, Galadria as a whole was a very peaceful realm, and that the House of Shadowray alone seemed to start most of the major disputes in court, having at one time or another feuded with all the other ruling families.

In his culture class, he was fascinated to learn that Earth music was very popular in Galadria, and made certain types of Galadrian flowers move and shake their leaves and stem in rhythm...in essence, dance! Peter shared his newfound knowledge with Monty.

"If I remember correctly, sir, you still haven't seen the manor's flower gardens yet."

"Oh yeah, I forgot." said Peter. "Are there a lot of Galadrian plants there?"

"Oh yes, sir," said Monty, cheerily. "Quite a number actually, and even a few of the famous Galadrian dancing flowers you've mentioned. We have Discoed Daisies, Rockaway Roses and a few patches of Tangoed Tulips."

"Do they really dance?"

"Enthusiastically, in fact. If you'd like, sir, tomorrow being Sunday, I think an afternoon in the flower gardens would be enjoyable."

"Sure, sounds like fun," Peter replied, looking forward to a change of pace.

The next day, after breakfast, Peter had to stifle his laughter when Monty returned to his room wearing a huge straw hat.

"Can't be too careful, sir," said Monty, generously applying sun block on top of his nose. "Sun damage is quite hazardous, you know. I've also taken the liberty of bringing another hat for you."

To Peter's horror, Monty pulled out an equally enormous straw hat that was folded neatly under his arm.

"Oh...no Monty, that's okay," he said, as Monty plopped the immense hat on his head. Peter felt like they were wearing beach umbrellas. "Aren't these hats a bit much?"

"Nonsense, sir," Monty replied, pulling out two pairs of big, black sunglasses and handing one of them to Peter. "I think they're quite fetching."

So off they went, through the halls and into the gardens, both wearing their gigantic sun gear. Peter walked along, feeling like a giant mushroom. They descended down many winding trails, as the foliage around them became wild and unkempt, reminding Peter of the unruly area surrounding Willowbrook Lake.

After about an hour of hiking, Peter found himself in the middle of a very strange forest. Huge, towering evergreen trees dominated the area, while patches of unusual flora grew randomly around the uneven ground. Smooth green leaves, larger than he was, were unfolding everywhere, as ladybugs the size of watermelons lazily crossed his path.

"Monty, are these the flower gardens? I was expecting a bunch of rose bushes and a fountain. It feels like we got lost in the wild."

"It does need a bit of trimming, doesn't it, sir," said Monty, crouching down and inspecting a particularly bright patch of small red roses. "Look at these flowers, sir. These are the famed Rockaway Rose species."

"They seem pretty normal to me. Guess they don't get much music down here."

Out of nowhere, Monty burst loudly into song, belting an odd fusion between a light ballad and heavy metal. As Peter looked on, he saw the roses slowly start to move. Their leaves were rolling in gentle waves, and they seemed to be dancing the hula.

"That's so cool," he said loudly, over Monty's ambitious solo, which ended on a rather high, squeaky note.

"Why thank you, sir."

"There sure are a lot of old trees here," Peter remarked, gazing up at all the endless treetops that seemed to continue growing defiantly past the clouds. "I've never seen trees this tall."

"Oh yes, sir," said Monty, peering up at the evergreens. "Most of these trees are ancient. I believe they were thriving here before the manor was even built. Magnificent, aren't they?"

"Yeah, they are. They're almost as big as the ladybugs."

"Well, those I'm afraid, are most definitely Galadrian. The ladybugs native to Earth are tiny in comparison, bit of a shock to me when I first saw one. Some people in Galadria keep them as pets, but although pretty, they're rather moody and ..."

As Monty continued, Peter gazed absentmindedly at the forest around them. Something had shifted. A flock of bluebirds flew quickly away from where they were situated, as if suddenly startled. Aside from Monty's voice, the forest had become unnaturally silent.

"...so droll, you know, sir. I mean really, they're insects, and..."

"Shhh," said Peter, peering intently at the dense patch of forest behind them. Now that Monty had stopped speaking, Peter realized how eerily quiet the forest had become. All the hairs on the back of his neck and arms had risen. Something was out there. Both he and Monty were standing completely still. It felt as if the slightest movement would set off some kind of chain reaction. Slowly, Peter reached for his boomerang...

"No, sir," whispered Monty, his hand on Peter's arm. "We must go back to the manor at once. Go on, back the way we came. I shall follow behind you."

"But Monty ..."

"Now, sir," he replied, slowly taking off his enormous hat and sunglasses.

Peter hesitantly started walking back up the path they had just taken, also removing his hat and sunglasses.

As soon as both of them were far enough away, Monty was again at Peter's side. Both of them walked briskly in silence. It was only when they had reached the manor that they spoke.

"What do you think that was?" asked Peter.

"I'm not sure, sir, but it was best that we came back to the manor. It could have been anything; the garden is full of animals. I've just never encountered one in that area before."

"Yeah, probably just an animal," Peter replied, although he thought the idea of Monty rushing them back up to the manor because an animal scared away some birds was rather extreme.

"Better safe than sorry, I always say," said Monty. "Besides, now would be an excellent opportunity to visit the library and read up on all the vegetation we saw."

And for the rest of the day that's exactly what they did. Peter was very impressed with the library. It was five levels of endless rows of high, dark wood shelves filled with every kind of book imaginable. There were also shelves packed full of old maps, globes, journals and scrolls, all piled on top of each other. As he and Monty were flipping through some books on the third floor, Mr. Frank was on the first floor, sitting at a cluttered table, pouring over stacks of dusty looking journals, mumbling to himself.

"Reading up on vegetation, are yeh?"

"Yes, Mr. Frank." Peter replied.

"WHAT?"

"I SAID, YES MR. FRANK."

"Yes what?"

"YES, WE'RE READING ON VEGETATION."

"So?"

"Nevermind, Mr. Frank."

"WHAT?"

"NEVERMIND!"

✳ ✳ ✳

That night, after Monty had left with his dinner tray, Peter was sitting on his bed in his mismatched pajamas, and he started going over in his mind what had happened in the forest. Oddly enough though, nothing actually happened. But try as he might, he still couldn't dismiss what he had felt.

"Probably just a huge ladybug in the bushes," he mumbled to himself, as he leaned over to turn off his bedside lamp. "Just some harmless forest creature that was frightened by our hats..."

And with that last thought, he settled into his cozy bed and effortlessly yawned himself to sleep.

WHAM!

Peter opened his eyes and sat up with a jolt. His room was completely dark, except for the pale moonlight streaming in from the high arched windows. He reached out and switched on his lamp. Someone was trying to break down his door!

"Who's there?" he yelled, grabbing his boomerang from the cushioned bench at the end of his bed. No one answered.

WHAM!

His door sounded like it was being hit with a battering ram, the thunder from the impact echoed in his room. Quickly, he reached over and pressed the silver button on the wall above his bedside table, then jumped over to the other side of his bed, near the windows.

Staring intently at his door and clutching his boomerang tightly in his hand, Peter started to hear the same strange noises again, like gusts of wind howling through the hall. This time, however, they were accompanied by a high-pitched screeching, the likes of which he had never heard. Then silence. The only sound he could hear was his own shallow breathing.

He was staring at the handle of his door, waiting to see if it would turn. The silence was almost deafening, then the door swung open.

"AHHHHHH!" yelled Monty, ducking quickly. Peter's boomerang had nearly taken his head off.

"Stay down, Monty!" Peter yelled. "It comes ba...."

But it was too late. Monty had stood back up and was sharply hit by the returning boomerang. Peter was surprised that, despite this, it still landed firmly in his hand.

"Monty, are you okay?" he asked, scrambling over his bed and kneeling down next to him. Monty was wearing a dark blue robe and was on one knee, massaging the back of his head.

"Sir, are you alright?" he asked, standing up, still massaging his head. "What happened?"

Peter quickly shut the door behind them.

"It happened again!" he said excitedly. "Someone was trying to break in here, but this time they didn't knock. It sounded like they were trying to ram down the door! And then I heard that noise again, like wind...and screeching! If Knor can't even get inside the manor, who else would be trying to smash their way into my room?"

It was almost morning when Peter had repeated what had happened, for what seemed like the twelfth time, to Aunt Gillian. They were in the formal sitting room next to the council chamber where they had first met. Aunt Gillian was wearing a long, light golden robe, while Peter was still in his mismatched pajamas. Mrs. Smith and Monty, both in dark blue robes, were standing stiffly next to the closed hall door.

"I don't see how Knor could've done it," said Aunt Gillian, pacing back and forth. "There's no way he could have gotten past Hillsides defenses. But you're right Peter, no one else would have any reason to break into your room."

"Could it be someone at the manor already?" he asked, leaning forward in his cushioned chair.

"I'm not certain, but I don't think so," she answered, "Everyone hired to work at Hillside goes through a thorough background check. Our entire staff has been working here a very long time."

"Well, it's a good thing Monty showed up when he did," said Peter, nodding towards Monty. "Whoever it was got scared away. But what were all those strange sounds, the wind...and that screeching?"

"I didn't move you when this happened the first time," she replied, "Because the room you're in was specially constructed, and is being guarded by very rare and powerful Galadrian objects. It's one of the safest rooms in the manor. The door, windows and their frames are lined with the same materials as your boomerang, not many forces could scratch it, much less break it down. Also, the noises you heard, the wind and the screeching, those are not coming from the person ramming your door."

"Where are they coming from then?"

"The tapestries in the hall," she continued, "Most of them are just normal tapestries made here on Earth, but a few of them are Galadrian, they're called Danjanestries, and are extremely rare. The one in front of your room is made from the feathers of Galadrian giant eagles. If anyone outside the room is forcibly trying to enter, or presents a significant danger to the person staying in the room, whether or not they are present, a Danjanestry will appear from the tapestry to protect you. You heard it screeching, and its wings beating made sounds like wind.

"A giant eagle is protecting my room?" he asked, making sure he was getting this right.

"Yes. Just like a giant Galadrian black panther is protecting this room."

"Aunt Gillian, if these tapestry Dangapastries...

"Danjanestries,"

"Danga..."

"There's no 'g', Dan-jan-es-tries."

"Danga..."

"Dan-jan..."

"Danga..."

"Stop saying 'Danga',"

"Uhh...Dan..jan...pastries?"

"You got half of it."

"Well...if I'm being guarded by a giant eagle," Peter continued, "Then whoever keeps trying to get to me must be pretty powerful to be able to fight it off. I mean, who would risk being attacked by a giant eagle? Twice!"

"Not many, but my sources assure me that Knor is still in Galadria. Also, the portal that leads to our council room from The Great Palace in Galadria hasn't been used and is constantly under heavy guard."

"I bet Knor has a portal to Hillside that no one knows about! A secret portal! And I bet I know where it is, the forest!"

"What forest?"

"Oh...um...the flower gardens!"

"Oh!" said Aunt Gillian. "Why there?"

"When we were there yesterday, everything suddenly became really quiet and eerie. It was weird. It felt like we were being watched," he said, leaning so far forward he was about to fall off his chair.

"I don't know," she said doubtfully. "Knor has never been past the council room into the manor. He's constantly with the council members, trying to build alliances and make them see his way. Also, portals are very rare. They're not a common means of transport like cars or boats. Most Galadrians outside the ruling families have probably never even seen one. They're extremely difficult to make and take an enormous amount of time and money to assemble. Only a few of the most prominent families have them, and they're all registered with the Supreme Council."

"So then...what happens now?" asked Peter.

"We can't let this rattle us," said Aunt Gillian confidently. "I know it must have been startling, but remember, whoever it was, was not able to enter your room. If the room's occupant is in danger, the door seals itself shut until the threat is gone. At such times, only you can open it. I think it would be best if you stayed where you were. Your location in the manor was already a secret that was obviously found out. To move you again would be pointless. I'll station one of the Royal Guards outside your door. In the meantime, Mrs. Smith and Montgomery will head a search of Hillside for any sign of an illegal portal, although a venture like that will take some time. Meanwhile, you must continue your lessons and prepare for the next rite. Montgomery will not leave your side during the day. We'll also alert the rest of the staff, there's no use keeping anyone in the dark anymore. Carry your Protava and Creamers with you, not that I have to remind you. I see you have your book bag and boomerang even now."

"I'm gonna finish these rites," said Peter determinedly. "I won't give Knor the satisfaction of scaring me away."

"I know you'll finish, but please do be careful. I'll notify the council of the attempted break in. I can't outright accuse Knor in court, but I can alert everyone to what's happened. Believe me, they'll suspect Knor just as much as we do."

8

THE MOONS OF DESTRITOR

On the surface, life in the manor continued in much the same way for Peter, with a few slight alterations. He attended his lessons regularly, except that now, a golden-armored guard stood outside his room and accompanied him and Monty everyday to the barren study room. Mr. Frank barely noticed the guard, while

Ms. Homebody welcomed him enthusiastically, offering him some of her mother's homemade chocolate chip cookies, though only after asking Monty first. And Ben was absolutely thrilled to meet a Royal Guard.

The guard's name was William, and although he was very polite, Peter noticed he didn't really like to talk much. In fact, he didn't like to talk at all. Monty informed Peter that it was because all eight of the golden armored guards were the official protectors of the queen and the Willowbrook family. They took their jobs very seriously and liked to stay quiet and focused at all times. It was probably for this reason that William politely refused to let Ben borrow his sword, despite his repeated pleas.

"...but I've heard that the Royal Guard's swords are some of the sharpest ever made, if I could just..."

"I'm afraid it really is against protocol, sir," William told him politely while tightening his grip on the sword.

"Just let me see it...here, cut this branch." Ben continued.

"I really shouldn't, sir."

"Just a small branch?"

"I shouldn't."

"How about you 'accidentally drop' the sword and I'll pick it up and give it back to you?"

"Sir, I'm going to have to ask you to step away..."

While everyone got used to having William around and guarding him, Peter noticed that since the night of the attempted break in, Monty was much more alert, and seemed to be taking his role as guardian more seriously. Peter had the feeling that he was upset at himself at the thought of an assailant loose in the manor, even though Peter reminded him that his swift arrival was what probably scared whoever it was away. He also figured that Monty must be exhausted, fulfilling both his regular duties, and organizing the search of the entire manor and its grounds for an illegal portal. After his lessons, everyone insisted that Peter stay in his room, as well as take all his meals there, at least until the search was over. Peter didn't really mind this, especially after his long, arduous lessons and strenuous Protava training. He would just lie on his bed and wonder about the next rites and what adventurous challenges they would be.

✳ ✳ ✳

The busy days passed quickly and Peter was once again facing the entire Galadrian court, anxiously awaiting his second rite. A rush of whispers echoed through the crowd as he made his way through the council room, William following closely behind him. William stood nearby as he stopped beside Aunt Gillian and bowed to the council. The Pollana was again centered in front of the throne and was teeming with an abundance of glowing light.

"Ladies and gentlemen of the court," Aunt Gillian began. "Before we proceed with the second Rite of Passage, there is an important piece of information you, as Galadrians, should know. I'm sure you've already heard the rampant rumors that the successor, Peter Willowbrook Huddleston, came into danger at Hillside Manor. Unfortunately, these rumors are true. As I have already informed the Supreme Council, a few days after the successor had triumphantly completed the first rite in front of us all, an unknown assailant attempted to force their way into the successor's bed chamber in the middle of the night, awakening the chamber's Danjanestry."

A outcry rose from the assemblage. Already, many members of the court were glaring at Knor, including Peter. Knor stood seemingly relaxed, completely unaffected by the glares and whispers.

"As you all know," continued Aunt Gillian, "the Danjanestry is only awakened if the occupant of the room is in immediate mortal danger. Thankfully, the assailant was sent scurrying away from the room's impenetrable entrance as the successor's guardian approached, even though the successor himself was in the chamber, Protava firmly in hand, ready to come face to face with this loathsome, obviously incompetent coward."

Aunt Gillian had distinctly said that last part while facing Knor. And while he continued to remain icily calm, Peter noticed his hands tighten on the sides of the golden podium in front of him.

"However, the court can be assured that this coward will be revealed. Willowbrook manor is being thoroughly searched, and as an added security,

Sir William Brandolf accompanies the successor on his daily schedule, and protects the successor's bed chamber. Sir William, one of our most esteemed Royal Guards, has been instructed to deal with threats to the successor with deadly force. I would like to note that despite this unfortunate turn of events, the successor has bravely kept to his schedule in a dedicated effort to secure Galadria. He is also, as we can all see, ready and eager to face his second Rite of Passage."

The court gave Peter a supportive round of applause. Before long however, Knor gestured to Lord Grandon, indicating that he wished to address the court.

"You may speak, Knor of the House of Shadowray," said Lord Grandon.

"Let me just say," said Knor, in his cold, distinct drawl, "That on behalf of the House of Shadowray, I am very relieved that no harm has come to the rather vulnerable successor. I am, though, as a citizen of Galadria, appalled that he had to be in life threatening danger before any amount of security was allotted to him. The fact that a dangerous assailant can so freely roam so close to an unguarded child in the middle of the night, does not speak well of the running of the Willowbrook manor. I am thankful, as I am sure we all are, that however late, the successor is now seemingly secure. It is unsettling to know that the ruling House of Willowbrook, it seems, is not so impenetrable after all."

"Knor of Shadowray," said Aunt Gillian, "your concerns, while predictably inaccurate, are noted. While your address has been heard, it does seem rather unnecessary, as I am sure court and council alike are very well aware of what your feelings are towards the successor. And since you are so concerned, I can guarantee you that when this coward is caught, you will be the first to become aware of it."

Knor gave a slight nod to Aunt Gillian, who simply looked at him momentarily, then turned to Lord Grandon.

"Lord Grandon," she continued, "Shall we begin the second rite?"

"Yes, your Majesty," Lord Grandon answered, slowly rising up from his seat and turning towards Peter. "The scepter is at the top of the mountain, along with another Pollana for your return. Be aware, you may only stop to rest for a few moments at a time, never longer, or you will have failed. Do you understand?"

Peter nodded. Lord Grandon turned towards the court.

"The successor will now step into the Pollana for the second rite," he said ceremoniously.

Peter turned toward Aunt Gillian, who was smiling encouragingly at him, then stepped into the Pollana. The court fell silent as he slowly sank into the light.

Peter opened his eyes to find himself standing in front of an immense mountain that rose high up into the sky. A sky with three pale, round moons, he was startled to see. Stepping over the edge of the Pollana, he found himself on the floor of a rocky valley, the only greenery he could see was on the slopes of the intimidating mountain. It seemed a simple enough task, he thought, starting up a rocky trail...reach the top of the mountain, never stopping for more than a few moments to rest.

As he started up the mountain, boomerang firmly in hand, the trail seemed rather uneventful. As the minutes turned to hours, the sun miraculously intensified, making him feel hot and sticky.

"It's alright," he said to the listening court, cheerfully continuing up the increasingly steep mountain trail. "Bit of sun never hurt anybody."

But as hour after hour passed the scorching sun began to seriously burn him. He tried to ignore the searing rays and heat, but before long Peter was sunburned, thirsty and starting to get very tired. The steep trail began to die out and eventually disappeared. He found himself grabbing onto hot, jagged rocks and strenuously hiking up the mountain. Every time he glanced up, the mountaintop didn't seem the slightest bit closer. He desperately wanted to stop and rest, just for a few minutes, but he knew that if he did, he would break his momentum, and despite himself, might not be able to continue climbing again.

Still more time passed, and Peter was beyond exhaustion. He was sure that he had been hiking the length of a day, yet the sun was still blazing overhead. His clothes were heavy, drenched with sweat, and he could hear his stomach grumbling violently with hunger. He needed to stop. Leaning against a narrow tree, he closed his eyes, and took a deep breath. With extreme effort he pulled himself painfully away from the intoxicating shade and forced himself to keep walking.

He was continuing his plodding progress up the mountain when Peter heard a faint buzzing noise. He shook his head to clear the noise, but it grew louder and louder, until...POKE! It felt like he had been hit on the side of the head with a dull ice pick.

"Ouch!"

Turning quickly, Peter saw two of the strangest looking birds he'd ever seen. They looked like extremely fat, round, red parrots with tiny wings and pointed yellow and orange beaks. For the life of him, he couldn't see how their little beating wings managed to carry their overstuffed, round bodies. They flew awkwardly side by side, only about a foot or two away from his head. POKE!

"Owww! Quit it!" he yelled, rubbing his forehead.

POKE!

"Ouch!"

Peter tried waving them away with his hands, but they didn't budge. Instead, they looked at him rather curiously, as if they couldn't understand why anyone would dislike being painfully poked on the head. He tried forcibly pushing them away, but it didn't work. They'd just happily flutter right back and...POKE! POKE!

"OUCH!!!" he yelled, two more red marks indented on his forehead.

Deciding on a change of tactic, Peter sprinted up the rocky mountainside. With those small wings, they'd never be able to keep up. He ran as fast as he could, for as long as he could, until, leaning momentarily against a large, mossy boulder, huffing and puffing, he was confident he'd lost them.

POKE! POKE!

"AHHHHH! That does it!" he said, rubbing his bruised, throbbing forehead and yelling at the two oblivious birds in front of him. Muttering furiously, he stuffed his boomerang into his pocket, and grabbed a fat bird by the beak in each hand, and bashed them against each other. To his dismay, and increasing frustration, they were unfazed by the violence. In fact, for a few idiotic seconds, they continued to voluntarily bash into each other, enjoying it immensely.

POKE! POKE!

"OWWWWW! Stop it!"

POKE! POKE!

"Fine!" he said, furiously, "How do you like it?"

Peter reached out and forcefully jabbed both of them on the head with his finger. This seemed to confuse them completely.

"Ohhhhh...you don't like that, do you?" he said, taking a quick step towards them.

"Well, too bad!" he yelled, in a crazed voice, jabbing each bird repeatedly on the head. The birds fluttered quickly away as he frantically chased them, poking at them relentlessly.

"YES, I KNOW I'M RUNNING DOWN THE MOUNTAIN!" he shouted hysterically to the court, jabbing wildly in front of him.

After the startled birds flew nervously away, Peter grudgingly turned around and started slowly trudging back up the mountain again.

Hours later, his legs felt like lead weights and his forehead was marked with bumpy purple bruises; he noticed the sun had started to set and the sky was filling with dense, dark clouds. Starving and dizzy, Peter decided he had to eat a Creamer. Still barely moving up the path, he reached into his brown leather book bag, pulled out the polished wooden box and opened it.

There they were, his delicious chocolate Creamers. Peter's stomach growled loudly. He looked at them closely and decided to eat the round, light blue Creamer with the golden wing on it. Popping it wearily into his mouth, he hungrily bit down and was delighted to find it tasted exactly like milk chocolate filled with a very light, fluffy caramel. He thankfully swallowed the Creamer and put the polished wooden box back in his book bag.

Careful to keep moving forward, Peter wasn't sure what to expect. He knew Creamers lasted an hour, and was hoping this one would give him the ability to fly. Half expecting to sprout wings from his back, he was alarmed to find nothing was happening. Suddenly he felt the strangest sensation overcome him. Then, peering down at his shoes, he realized he was slowly floating off the ground!

"I-I'm flying," he said excitedly.

After a few moments of utter astonishment, Peter realized he was not flying. He seemed to be hovering about a foot off the ground, and try as he might to move, he just sort of floated there. Every so often, gusts of wind would push him back and forth. Putting his hands straight in front of him, flapping his arms, kicking his legs...nothing seemed to propel him anywhere. He just hovered, like a half inflated balloon. Then, concentrating very hard on a tree in front of him...he began to glide slowly towards it. It worked!

"Alright, I don't flap my arms or anything...I just concentrate on where I want to go," he said excitedly.

Focusing on a boulder about fifty feet away from him, Peter continued to glide smoothly forward, never rising higher than a foot or two off the ground. It wasn't until he switched his focus to a tree branch protruding out from a cliff above him that he slowly started to rise higher and higher into the air. He noticed, halfway up the cliff, that strong gusts of wind would scarily blow him off course and that he would have to concentrate extra hard on where he wanted to go. This was going great, he thought, as he concentrated on the next cliff above him. After an hour of this, he would be much closer to the top.

Peter hovered past level after level of rocky mountain. The dimming sun slowly disappeared, and the night sky was filled with the bright, pale light that reflected from its three round moons. As sun fell, the scorching heat of the day was replaced by night air that was surprisingly cold and sharp. Feeling it had been close to an hour since he ate his Creamer, Peter cautiously continued rising up the levels of the mountain, staying as close as he could to its steep, rocky walls.

Peter felt something ice cold splash on his head, then his shoulders, and before he could think twice, it had started to rain. Raindrops the size of apples pelted his body, and within seconds he was soaked to the bone in freezing water. Straining to concentrate, he was halfway up a cliff when his focus waned. He was feeling heavier by the second.

"Uh...oh," he said, looking down at the four story drop below him.

Trying hard not to be distracted by the heavy raindrops crashing against his face, he looked up and focused all his concentration on the ledge above him. It must have been about ten feet away. Floating slowly upwards, he continued focusing on the ledge, and he reached out pulling himself up, cutting his hands on the jagged mountain wall in front of him. The Creamer was wearing off startlingly fast.

Peter was concentrating so hard he thought his head would burst. Yet he was hardly moving upward. Scrambling against the rocky wall, he finally got both his arms over the ledge, when his legs dropped heavily from under him. He yelled as he dug his fingers into the earth, the weight of his legs dragging him off the cliff. He hung motionless clinging to the cliff with his arms. His legs were dangling horrifically. He was terrified that his strength would give out, and he'd plunge off the mountain.

He gradually calmed his nerves and managed to dig his toe into a groove. Slowly he pulled himself onto the ledge. Huffing and puffing, Peter lay sprawled out on the muddy ground. Forcing himself to stand, his knees shaking violently under him, he started stumbling up the trail. With every step, he felt himself getting weaker, as icy winds and heavy drops of rain continued to work tirelessly against him.

By now, Peter was nearly crawling up the mountain. He had not expected his second rite to be nearly this difficult. It was relentless, it was cruel, and unlike his first rite, it was unbelievably long and drawn out. This challenge required him to dig into a deeper part of himself, the part of him that refused to give up. Rationalizing his situation had stopped helping him. He was too tired and beat up to think at all. All that was left was for him to keep going, and to refrain from telling himself the reasons he wouldn't make it.

Peter kept slipping on the steep, muddy trail, his body feeling numb and empty. All he could do was keep picking himself back up and moving forward. It wasn't until he turned a rocky corner and saw another series of endless trails winding up the mountain that he reached into his book bag for another Creamer. It was both hunger and desperation that made him reach for the polished wooden box. He was starving.

With trembling fingers, Peter opened the small box and hungrily peered at the eleven chocolate Creamers in front of him. He resisted a strong urge to just start stuffing them all into his mouth. Instead, too tired to even try and guess what they did, he chose a plump Creamer from the corner of the box. It looked like it was made of transparent stone, like a small, blue crystal made of sugar. On it were little yellow stars and a moon. He stuffed it emphatically into his mouth and pushed the closed box back into his book bag. It tasted like strong licorice and was very chewy, despite its crystal-like appearance. He would have liked it even if it had tasted like liver.

He resumed his stagger up the never ending mountain and waited anxiously for something to happen, hoping whatever did would speed his trek up the path in front of him. But nothing happened. Several long minutes went by with no change to his current state. Thankfully, it had stopped raining, and the dark, imposing sky had started to clear. After what seemed like an hour, the Creamer still hadn't taken effect. Maybe it was a dud?

Peter looked up and saw that the sky had cleared, and as one last patch of clouds moved murkily through, three round moons were once again shining brightly onto the mountainside. As he stepped into a clearing Peter began to feel something strange happening. He was bathed in pale moonlight, and as he looked up at the mysterious moons, he felt his clammy body grow even colder. Eyes widening, he clenched his hands into fists in a vain effort to try and steady himself.

Suddenly, his mind was bombarded with an avalanche of bizarre thoughts and random images. His eyes involuntarily clamped shut, as his hands raced to his temples. An explosion of information threatened to burst his head wide open. Peter winced, feeling sharp pains all over his body, and then, mercifully, his mind became completely clear. He opened his eyes, and felt his breath escape him. He was standing in complete darkness. As he turned, looking for any clue to where he was, he instinctively jumped back. Sitting in front of him was a large, white tiger, staring at him peacefully. The tiger bared its fangs and growled menacingly. Looking above him, all Peter saw was red, until he heard a loud, deep wailing noise from behind. Turning around, the same tiger sat staring straight at him, purring loudly.

Peter opened his eyes. He was on the mountain trail gazing up at the sky. The pale moonlight was still shining down on him, as he felt his entire body start to shake, almost convulse, as the effects of the Creamer slowly faded away. Kneeling in the mud, he was dumbstruck at what had just happened. Was it a dream? A premonition? Even if it was, it didn't make any sense.

He quickly stood up and pushed himself to start walking. His hands were trembling, from shock or cold, he wasn't sure.

As the hours passed, he decided he would have to forget about the tiger...at least for now. All his remaining energy had to go towards reaching the top of the mountain. Step after agonizing step, he moved forward, until finally, momentously, he reached the mountaintop.

Peter saw the gold scepter lying on a round, dark, smooth stone. Next to it was the Pollana. He was stunned; he thought he was hallucinating. Without so much as a glance behind him, he staggered towards the scepter and clutched it in his shaking hand. The Pollana started to swirl with a glowing light that illuminated the shadowy mountaintop. A surge of relief washed over him. It had started to rain again, and as he stepped into the light, the gold scepter in his hand, he felt his body collapse from under him.

Peter lay sprawled on the floor. He looked up to see the entire Galadrian court staring at him intensely. There were no applause though, and the room was silent. Slowly, he turned his aching head and saw Knor gazing coldly at him from behind his golden podium. Seeing Knor's self-righteous face filled him with one thought...stand up. He tried, but his knees were violently shaking. Taking a deep breath, he steadied himself and slowly stood up, the gold scepter clutched in his hand. As he faced the court, he raised the scepter above his head and managed a very weak smile.

The crowd burst into wild applause, hooting and cheering as they stood from their seats. Many of them looked very tired. Peter felt a warm hand on his shoulder helping him step out of the Pollana, then raising his arm back into the air.

"Peter Willowbrook Huddleston," said Aunt Gillian loudly, as she hung onto his arm, "Has returned to us bearing the Scepter of Perseverance. He has overcome incredible odds and has shown outstanding determination and will."

Peter, feeling a gentle squeeze on his arm, handed the gold scepter to Lord Grandon. The councilman placed it carefully into the crystal ceremonial case next to the scepter from his first challenge.

"I am now proud to declare the second Rite of Passage...complete!"

Aunt Gillian proclaimed, as the court roared with applause. "Peter, bow to the council and follow me," she whispered.

Peter bowed carefully and then followed his aunt through the open section of the wall beside her throne. Entering, he saw Monty waiting for him, several silver containers assembled on the table in front of him. As the door slid closed behind him, Peter started shaking from head to toe.

"Are you okay?" asked Aunt Gillian concernedly, as she and Monty led him to the cushioned bench in front of Monty's table.

"Yeah, I'm okay," he answered breathlessly, gratefully sitting down. He saw his distorted reflection on a polished silver box and could tell he looked horribly beat up. His face was as pale as chalk, heavy dark circles hung under his eyes and his forehead was covered in dark purple bruises where those two round, red birds had repeatedly poked him. Monty lifted his book bag from across his chest and placed it on the polished table. Peter, shaking worse by the second, managed to take off his own muddy, soaking wet shirt. He was immediately wrapped in thick, warm, quilted blankets. Monty picked up a silver teapot and poured hot tea into a deep golden bowl.

"You must drink this, sir," said Monty importantly, steadying the golden bowl in Peter's shaking hands.

"Okay..." he said wearily, breaking out in a delirious smile. Holding the warm bowl under his chin with both hands, he could feel the hot steam on his clammy face. He slowly drank the tea and found it was very hot and tasted like honey and eucalyptus. He could feel his chest warm rapidly, like he was submerged in a hot bath. He noticed that as he drank, his hands and body gradually stopped shaking, and as he gratefully drained the bowl to the last drop, he felt as though he had eaten an entire hot meal. Although still exhausted, he felt his strength slowly returning.

"This is amazing," said Peter, handing the bowl back to Monty.

"It's Galadrian honey tea," said Aunt Gillian, wrapping him in another thick blanket. "We've found that Galadrian honey is miraculously healing here on Earth...the color's already returning to your face."

"Ouch...oh that feels good..." said Peter, as Monty started dabbing ointment onto his bumpy forehead. "How long was I climbing that mountain?"

"The days in Destritor, the realm you were in, last much longer than here." she replied, "You haven't stopped climbing in about a day and a half."

"A day and a h-half?" he said, feeling dizzy again.

"You did so well," his aunt continued, handing him another bowl of hot honey tea. "We were all very impressed, especially with the way you managed to use your first Creamer. Although it did give me a start when it wore off and you were left hanging over that ledge...I almost called off the rite. Thank goodness you managed to pull yourself up."

"Oh yeah... I remember...that," said Peter, between large gulps of tea, "But did you see...what happened...when I ate...that second Creamer?"

"Yes, it was strange, nothing seemed to happen." she continued, taking back his empty bowl.

"Until awhile later," Peter added, as Monty proceeded to clean and bandage the cuts and scrapes covering his hands.

"I didn't notice anything..." she replied, "The only thing I saw was that about an hour later you stopped and looked up at Destritor's three moons, then you knelt down on the trail. I figured you were exhausted."

"You didn't see all those images, all those...those visions? It felt like I was transported somewhere else."

"Transported?" she asked concernedly. "You only looked up at the moons for a few seconds. What did you see?"

"It was a tiger..."

"A tiger?"

"It was a white tiger," Peter continued, excitedly. "Aunt Gillian...it was Rune."

9

RUNE

The next day, Peter was sleeping deeply in his comfy bed as the morning's light warmed his blankets. Insistent tapping at his door awakened him.

"Sir?" whispered Monty, poking his head into the room. "Are you awake yet?"

"Hmmm...Morning...Monty," Peter groggily answered, his face buried in his pillow.

He was still warmly bundled in the thick quilted blankets Aunt Gillian had wrapped him in the night before. After telling her what he could remember of his visions under Destritor's moons, he drank as much honey tea as he could hold and waited for the court to return to Galadria before walking wearily back to his room with Monty and William. Aunt Gillian was just as puzzled by his visions as he was. And she instructed Monty to have Rune found and brought back to the manor. Meanwhile, Peter changed into his pajamas and fell asleep the second he collapsed on his bed.

"I've brought your breakfast, sir," Monty said cheerily, as he placed the tray on Peter's bed. "And since I'm sure you're very hungry, I've prepared quite a large meal."

Peter slowly opened his eyes. He didn't want to move...ever. He was so warm and comfortable cocooned in his thick blankets that he felt he could have spent the rest of his life there. But he knew he had to get up eventually, and Monty was right, he was starving. His entire body felt extremely sore. Every one of his muscles was tired and achy.

"Owww..." he moaned, as he stretched his arms and legs and slowly sat up.

"Still sore, sir? Well, that's to be expected. You know what would help that? A good, hot bath."

"Oh, that's okay," said Peter, stuffing sausage and hash browns into his mouth.

"Are you sure, sir? After all, you still have your lessons today," said Monty brightly.

"On second thought, a bath sounds really good," he said thoughtfully, biting into a large, plump blueberry muffin. The thought of sitting through his long lessons, followed by hours of Protava training made a hot bath seem like a really great idea.

"I shall draw your bath water immediately, sir," said Monty, walking towards the bathroom.

"Hey Monty," Peter said, after pouring himself a cup of very hot, hot chocolate. "Am I going to see Rune today?"

"I should suspect so, sir," said Monty, from the bathroom, speaking loudly over the sound of running water. "Rune has always walked freely around the grounds. Right now Ben is looking for him and will bring him to your Protava training this afternoon."

"Alright," said Peter, as he gulped his hot chocolate. "How is the search going? Find any sign of a portal yet?"

"No, not yet, sir," said Monty, stepping out of the bathroom. "We're covering the manor very thoroughly though, and should be done fairly soon. Then we shall proceed to the grounds."

"There must be an illegal portal. How else would someone be able to break into a place like this?"

"Very true sir, but not to worry, if there's an illegal portal here at Hillside, we'll be sure to find it," said Monty, as he carefully removed the bandages around Peter's hands. "Excellent, that honey ointment has already healed your cuts."

"I could help...with the search."

"Oh, no sir," said Monty quickly, as if this was a shocking idea. "You must concentrate on your lessons."

"Okay, just a thought."

"We couldn't let you endanger yourself while a possible threat is loose on the grounds. Now, I shall be off. Sir William is standing at the door, and once your bath is full, the taps will turn themselves off. If that will be all, I shall be back within the hour to fetch you for your lessons. By the way, sir, forgive me for saying, but well done yesterday. We are all exceedingly proud."

"Thanks, Monty."

"Of course, sir."

And with that, Monty left the room, shutting the door behind him.

Just as Peter finished eating his copious breakfast, he heard the sound of running water stop, and lazily made his way towards the bathroom. Steam was rising from the sparkling surface of a bath as large as a small swimming pool, beckoning Peter. Monty had left a fluffy blue towel and a pair of slippers on the corner of the bath. Peter took off his mismatched pajamas and slowly stepped into the hot pool. Sitting down on a smooth ledge, the hot water reached just above his chin. He was amazed at how good it felt. All the aching and soreness just melted away. But even as Peter felt more and more relaxed, his mind churned trying to understand the mysterious visions. What could they mean? Why would he envision Rune? Why had the sky turned red? And what was that deep wailing he heard?

Peter started thinking about the Creamer that had caused the trance. It had a moon and stars on it and seemed to be triggered by the moonlight that night. Maybe it malfunctioned since Destritor had three moons, he thought. Maybe it's supposed to be used on a world with only one moon. At any rate, the only thing he felt sure about was that the vision centered on...Rune.

With that conclusion, his mind slowed its furious pace, and he relaxed. Peter was just dozing off when he heard Monty return to his room.

"Sir, are you ready yet?" said Monty, from the hall door. "It's almost time. Should I return in a few minutes?"

"Yeah...sorry. I didn't realize how long I've been in here. I'll be ready soon."

Peter rushed into his clothes and began another long day of political and culture studies. His tutors were exceedingly happy, and relieved, that he had passed his second rite. The excitement, however, was short lived, as they insisted on not losing a moment of his class time. Mr. Frank decided to give him a surprise test on the differences and similarities between the royal houses, while Ms. Homebody had asked Madam Cornhen to stop by to join them in sampling an assemblage of assorted, homemade Galadrian sweets that she wanted Peter to experience.

"Master Huddleston, Madam Cornhen, you must try this!" said Ms. Homebody giddily, pointing to one of over twenty desserts covering her desk. It looked like a clear bubble the size of a bowling ball was clinging to a glass plate.

"What is it?" Peter asked curiously. "I don't want to pop it."

"Oh Jessica, you made Zvella! It's my favorite!" said Madam Cornhen happily. "You should try it Master Huddleston, it's a delicacy and very difficult to make. Eat it as you would ice cream. Don't worry. Although it looks like a bubble, it won't pop. Go ahead, try it."

"Alright," said Peter, and he, Madam Cornhen and Ms. Homebody dug their spoons into the jiggly bubble. Peter was surprised at the Zvella's texture, and he could not feel any weight on his spoon. Despite the three large spoonfuls they had scooped, the remaining dessert on the plate did not pop. It jiggled and reshaped itself into another smaller bubble.

"Mmmmmm," swooned Madam Cornhen, around the spoon in her mouth.

Peter tried the unusual dessert and was amazed by it. It smelled lightly of lavender, and it was like biting into air. The flavor was a surprise, and unmistakable. It tasted like cinnamon, vanilla, chocolate and mint, all at once. And when Peter swallowed it, he felt a ticklish tingling down his throat.

"This is fantastic!" he said, digging his spoon back into the bubble.

"Thank you," Ms. Homebody replied, blushing.

"Really, Jessica," said Madam Cornhen, "This is the best Zvella I've ever had. It's so light. The key to Zvella is its lightness. The lighter the better, and this is practically weightless."

"Oh, stop..." Ms. Homebody replied, waving her hand and turning a deep shade of scarlet. "It's just something I threw together for class. How do you like it Montgomery? I made yours special..."

Peter turned to see Monty at the doorway, a huge bubble the size of a watermelon bobbing precariously on the plate he was holding in front of him.

The Zvella was not Ms. Homebody's only treat for Peter to try. After enjoying all the delicious dishes of custards, crèmes, chocolates, and ices, Peter began to read out loud about Galadrian cuisine and discovered that he had just sampled many of the most popular, and most complicated desserts.

After a fantastic Galadrian culture lesson, Peter set out for his Protava lesson. And Ben made sure this one was one of his most grueling. He made Peter spend hours sprinting back and forth, hurling his boomerang while performing several different strength and speed exercises that were absolutely exhausting.

After his intense workout, Peter shuffled back to his room, escorted as usual by Monty and William. Peter was concerned when Ben told him that Rune was nowhere to be found on the grounds.

✳ ✳ ✳

His lessons and training over the next few days passed in this same manner. While Peter remained as diligent as ever with his training, he was distracted by his conviction that Knor had a secret portal into Hillside. That conviction was not dimmed by the lack of results from the searches of the manor. And, of just as much concern to Peter, was that Rune remained missing. The extensive search of Hillside Manor's grounds turned up no sign of the white tiger.

Peter's distraction turned into concern over the lack of results. He thought he had waited long enough and, knowing time was of the essence, Peter decided to look for Rune himself. He must find out what his strange visions in Destritor meant.

"Thanks Monty...thanks William. I'm feeling pretty tired, so I think I'll go to bed early tonight," said Peter, opening his bedroom door.

"Would you like me to fetch your dinner now, sir?"

"No that's okay Monty, I'm really beat tonight."

"Not even a small supper? It will be ready in a moment."

"No, it's alright..."

"But..."

After assuring Monty he would buzz him if he felt hungry, Peter shut his door and started planning for his exploration. He decided to start looking for Rune in the animal preserve. As for escaping his bedroom, he was amazed to discover that William never left his post. All his meals were brought to him and Peter never opened his door without seeing him fully at guard. So slipping out through the hallway was out of the question.

While the door was closed to him, he was surprised to discover that his windows opened rather easily. Wanting to draw as little attention as possible to his escape route, he decided that he should not use his bed sheets to climb down the wall. Poking his head out of the window, he was happy to see that the vines growing on the manor walls were thick and would make an excellent ladder. He stepped out of his open window onto a very narrow ledge. As his hand left the perimeter of his room...SNAP! The window slammed shut! Desperate, Peter tried to open it, but it was no use, his windows were locked and the glass felt as strong as steel. Wondering how he was going to reenter his room, he continued to slowly climb down the thick vines to the garden below.

Committed to his search, Peter stumbled through the shadows cast by a bright moon toward the animal preserve. Even with the bright moonlight, he was relieved to see some lights left on for the animals. The last thing he wanted to do was wander up to a sleeping bear in the dark.

"Rune... Rune..." Peter quietly called out as he wandered amid the snoring monkeys and sleepwalking peacocks. He still could not get over how tame and domesticated these animals were. He froze as he stumbled upon a fierce looking leopard. Peter stared as the predator stealthily approached, he thought his heart would stop as the leopard thrust his head toward him. And he nearly collapsed with relief when the leopard licked his hand and lazily wandered away.

"Rune...Rune..." he continued, his heart still beating rapidly.

Peter searched and searched without hearing or seeing Rune. He paused and realized he had wandered into the grassy territory at the very back of the preserve. Peering through the thick, tall stalks of grass and leaves, he spotted a large pond a short distance away. But what really caught his eye was a large, worn hole in the preserve wall. As he looked close, the thick stone wall appeared to have been smashed in by a gigantic battering ram. Cautiously climbing through the hole, he found himself in the middle of a wilderness.

"The flower gardens!" Peter whispered to himself, as he continued to walk deeper into the dark, untamed forest.

"Rune..."

As he moved into the wild thickness, Peter heard a fierce growling a few feet away. He turned and saw Rune, half hidden in shadows, fangs bared, ready to pounce on him.

"Rune! Rune it's me!" cried Peter, the sight of an attacking tiger freezing him where he stood. But Rune didn't seem to recognize him; the tiger was ready to kill. Suddenly, from directly above Peter came a booming, wailing roar. Looking up, he saw red and recognized his vision on Destritor. He was stunned to stillness, Rune leaped on top of him, knocking him heavily to the ground. Peter tried to protect himself, curling up in a ball on the forest floor, the booming roars still deafening in his ears. But he didn't feel the pain of the tiger's claws ripping into him...Rune was not attacking him. Cautiously, he cracked an eye open and saw Rune viciously clawing and biting at a huge, massive boulder behind him! Rolling away and getting quickly to his feet, he identified the source of the booming howls. It was the only animal Monty had warned him about in the preserve...a hippo, the most gigantic, angriest looking hippo he could ever have imagined. With a shudder of terror he realized that when he had glanced up and saw red, he had stared into the giant creature's gaping, attacking mouth. He had to act fast. Next to the furious hippo, Rune looked like a house cat. Figuring his boomerang would be useless against an enraged beast of this size, he reached blindly inside his book bag for his Creamers. He grabbed the first Creamer he touched and stuffed it into his mouth swallowing quickly.

Nothing happened.

"Oh come on!" he yelled, jumping up and down, hoping to get it into his system faster. Rune was now on top of the rampaging hippo, biting uselessly at the place its neck should have been. "Hurry up!" he cried to himself, continuing his manic jumps.

Peter's erratic movements caught the hippo's attention. The angry hippo set its sights on him, ignoring the terrifying roar and ripping claws of the tiger dug onto its back. The giant beast charged, and Peter turned to run and...slipped. Just as the massive animal was about to crush him like a bug, he fell suddenly and rolled down the sloping ground away from the deadly attack. The creature smashed its head into the massive, ancient trunk of a tree just beside where Peter had slipped. He watched, the breath knocked out of him, as the hippo staggered backwards, howling in pain. The hippo turned back towards Peter, absolutely enraged. As the hippo was about to charge, the massive tree cracked. Rune leaped off the beast's back just before the dense tree trunk fell cracking heavily onto the hippo's head. The hippo collapsed, unconscious, sending a thick cloud of dirt and debris flying everywhere, and the forest was enveloped in silence.

Stunned, Peter sank to his knees. The hippo was knocked out! He couldn't believe it! Aware that it might recover quickly or that another one might be nearby, he called to Rune and the two of them sprinted back through the hole in the preserve wall, dashing through the animal preserve.

Panting from their sprint, they reached the manor walls and caught their breath. Bent over, his hands on his knees, Peter shook all over. He had found Rune, but he had no idea how they were going to get back into his room, much less unseen. His pulse back close to normal, Peter searched for a way into the manor. Amazingly, the first door he tried was unlocked! He didn't wait to question his good fortune and led Rune up a small stairway. His luck was holding, the stairway led them straight to the hall where his room was.

Almost there! But now he had to get past the ever-diligent William. He began running plausible excuses in his mind about why he was out of bed. He decided the best course was to walk boldly up to his room and see what happened. As he approached his room, he couldn't believe it! William had fallen asleep! Quietly he opened his bedroom door and he and Rune slipped in and silently closed it behind them. Dumbfounded and weary with relief, Peter sat on the floor and hugged the furry tiger tightly.

"Thanks buddy, you saved my life," said Peter gratefully. Rune gingerly licked his face. "Are you okay, boy?" he continued, checking Rune's fur to see if he was hurt. "That was the biggest animal I've ever seen! And we got away...I can't believe it! We got back into the manor too...I can't believe our luck!"

Peter stopped, his mouth dropped open as the thought came to him. He reached inside his book bag pulling out his box of Creamers. He slowly opened the polished box and confirmed his suspicion.

The Creamer he had eaten in the forest was the one shaped like a four leafed clover.

✳ ✳ ✳

In the morning, Peter told a perplexed Monty that Rune had scratched on his door in the middle of the night. An embarrassed and unusually sleepy William could not deny the story.

After thinking it through during the night, Peter assumed that Rune had been keeping an eye on the escaped hippos all this time. And though the question of whether or not Knor had a secret portal into the manor was still on his mind, he was relieved to know that his visions on Destritor had been a warning.

After an unusually quick breakfast, Monty mentioned that Ben, participating in the ongoing search of the grounds for an illegal portal, had located a hole in the preserve wall next to the hippo pond. Monty thought it was very lucky that they had left the flower gardens early during their outing.

"I keep telling Ben to build a separate, stronger wall around that pond. Those hippos have always been territorial and moody. They love trying to bash the preserve wall in. We're constantly reinforcing it. Imagine, giant hippos loose in the flower gardens! If anyone had gotten near the young in their pond...it makes me shudder to even think about it."

"They'd be pretty mad, huh Monty?"

"Oh yes sir. They'd be furious!"

Peter was surprised that he was happy that his lessons proceeded as usual, and he was ecstatic to discover that Rune had apparently decided to never leave his side.

"What in the name of...that's a big cat!" said Mr. Frank, as Rune sat down beside Peter during his political studies.

"This is Rune, he's..."

"Prune?"

"RUNE, MR. FRANK, HIS NAME'S RUNE."

"Who?"

"The tiger, his..."

"WHAT?"

"Nothing..."

Ms. Homebody, on the other hand, was absolutely delighted.

"Good afternoon everyone, I...oh my goodness, is that a tiger?" she enthused.

"Ms. Homebody, this is..."

"Rune! Of course! I've seen pictures of him with Her Majesty, she was much younger of course, but you know. I was looking through some books with mother, and she said, I remember like it was yesterday, she said, 'Jessie,' that's what mother calls me, Jessie. She said, 'Jessie, this is a picture of Queen Gillian, her pet tiger Rune...and Montgomery Clearwater.' That's the first time I ever saw a picture of our Montgomery...hmmmmm..."

"Ms. Homebody?"

"Yes?" she said, swooning.

"Nothing..."

✳ ✳ ✳

It seemed that time passed slowly. Buried in his preparation, Peter lost track of the days until his routine ended abruptly. And Peter found himself once again staring out at the Galadrian court, awaiting his third Rite of Passage.

"Good luck," said Aunt Gillian comfortingly, as Peter slowly sank into the swirling glow below him. "Don't worry, I know you'll be fine."

The last thing he saw were the concerned blue eyes of a worried looking Rune, following his decent into the light.

10

SOUL SEARCHING

When Peter opened his eyes, he found himself standing in a quiet, darkened room. The cool air around him smelled strongly of mint, which had a very calming effect on him. A younger boy was sitting on a large silk cushion in the middle of the chamber.

The boy was wearing a very long, elaborate, shimmering emerald green robe that spread out onto the floor. He was also completely bald, without the slightest trace of hair on his round, childlike face. His unusually long fingers were composed neatly on his lap. His appearance was unusual, but what really got Peter's attention were his eyes, which glowed brightly as they serenely considered Peter.

"Have a seat, Peter Willowbrook Huddleston," said the young man, in a deep, echoing voice, and gestured to a place in front of the large cushion he was sitting on.

Peter did so, his attention riveted by the glowing eyes.

"Welcome. I am Alexontorus. I am one of only two oracles in Galadria. It is my task to conduct you through the third rite.

"The third rite is considered to be the most difficult," the oracle said.

Peter slumped a little with the oracle's statement. 'Harder than climbing an unending mountain?' he thought. He tried to hide his concern, and returned the oracle's steady gaze.

Peter knew Alexontorus could sense his discomfort, and he tried to calm himself and prepare for this difficult test.

The oracle smiled at Peter's efforts and said, "The completion of your third rite will require you to pass a soul reading."

"What?" said Peter, unsure what this meant.

"I shall now begin."

"Wait! I..." he began, but already he felt numb.

The oracle had placed both his ethereal hands on the sides of Peter's head.

Peter stared, hypnotized, into the oracle's eyes. As he gazed into his blazing eyes they began to pulse with a blinding intensity. Peter's consciousness sank into the burning depths of light.

✳ ✳ ✳

"You have passed," said the oracle, releasing Peter's head, and his eyes calmed to their original spectral glow.

With a tight smile, he handed Peter a gold scepter from beneath his abundant emerald robe. Peter could sense the Pollana behind him as it filled with its own light.

"What? ... That's it?" mumbled Peter, having somewhat recovered from his trance-like state. He absently accepted the scepter from the oracle. "What else do I do? How did I pass?"

"This is the challenge of virtue, of moral excellence. There is nothing you could have done to pass this test except be who you are."

"That can't be all," said Peter, not knowing why he was questioning having passed.

"You would be surprised how many young nobility have managed to complete all the other rites, but have failed this one. In this trying time, it is a testament to your aunt's faith in you that she would approve this challenge. It also reveals what your adversaries truly think of your character. Were you a different kind of person, you would have failed."

Peter sat silently, considering the oracle's words, not quite sure he understood.

"Alright, thank you...sir," he said, as he slowly stood up and in a daze made his way to the glowing Pollana.

"Some advice, Peter Willowbrook Huddleston," said the oracle, suddenly, "I have seen you...your father...he loves you. You don't understand his silence towards you."

Peter was dumbfounded. Why was the oracle bringing up his father? And with the entire court watching them. He felt his throat tighten. He didn't know what to say. Why was he telling him this?

"Don't you see, child? You remind him of your mother, and he misses her...terribly."

Peter's eyes began to water. The oracle was answering the question that had been plaguing him in the back of his mind. He started to tremble.

"You must trust that he loves you. Too many brilliant children have fallen, not because of a lack of courage, or strength, or intelligence, but because of their inability to see how much they are truly valued by those around them. Things, and people, are not always as they seem."

"I miss him..." Peter stammered.

"I know," said the oracle, "Give him time, he will find his way...now go, they are waiting."

Holding the gold scepter, Peter stepped into the light and was standing in front of the Galadrian court. Although he saw this as the simplest challenge, in time he would understand it was, by far, the hardest rite he faced.

11

BAPTISM BY FIRE

After his third rite, Peter spent a lot of time thinking about what the oracle had told him. He was a little angry that his feelings toward his father were revealed to the court when he was still in that susceptible state. Yet he knew what was said was true, and he was grateful for the insight.

"He just wanted to make sure that you were aware of something really important that you were feeling," said Aunt Gillian, "He knew it would help you. The entire court was very impressed. Knor's suggestion for this challenge completely backfired on him. An oracle's soul reading is indisputable."

The days following passed in the same predictable pattern he had grown accustomed to. His tutors were thrilled he had passed his third rite, but quickly focused his attentions back toward the lessons. Peter could feel the tensions building. No one said anything aloud nor acted differently, but he could tell everyone in the manor was apprehensive about his fourth and final rite. The only Galadrian virtue left was courage, and he felt he would need every last bit of his to deal with whatever lay ahead.

Mr. Frank increased his political study time by almost double, while Ms. Homebody had taken to the habit of stuffing him with Galadrian sweets, insisting he keep his strength up. He wasn't sure, but he suspected that Ms. Homebody felt guilty that they hadn't covered the history and customs of Galadrian oracles in her class yet. Seeming to want to make up for it, she brought him, Monty, William and Rune to the history museum for his last cultural studies lesson. He appreciated the change, as the past few days had been spent laboring over several difficult tests in all three of his subjects. He was up for anything to take his mind off his fourth rite, which he was painfully aware was the next day.

Peter was surprised by the museum. Apparently it was not only dedicated to the history of Galadria, but of Earth's history and different cultures as well. He figured this was for the visiting dignitaries who frequently stayed at the manor.

"As you know, Master Huddleston, Madam Cornhen is our Galadrian and Earth historian and is responsible for running the museum!" Ms. Homebody bubbled.

"So good to see you again, Master Huddleston, I wasn't aware you'd be visiting us here today." said Madam Cornhen jovially, as they strolled through the exhibits. She was wearing the same gray dress suit and silver belt.

"I know...surprise! Just thought of it last minute!" said Ms. Homebody, with enough cheerfulness to knock over an elephant. "It was actually mother's suggestion. Last night, we were making cheesecake, mother loves cheesecake, but..."

"It's a pleasure, of course, Jessica." said Madam Cornhen. "I just would have liked to arrange more of a study plan. The museum is rather large...but I suppose a random walk through would suffice. We could plan for a specific area of interest on your next visit. By the way, Jessica, thank you so much for the tin of homemade peanut brittle, it was delicious."

"Oh I'm so glad you liked it! I'll tell mother, it's her recipe! I gave one to Master Huddleston, Monty, Mrs. Smith, William, Mr. Frank, though I don't think he liked it, Ben and...oh, um, where's Rune going?"

Peter hadn't noticed Rune wandering off.

"Your tiger," said Madam Cornhen, "He's beautiful, though I don't think he's usually allowed inside the museum, so many priceless artifacts."

"I promise Rune won't break anything, Madam Cornhen," said Peter, "He's always very well behaved. Rune...Rune..."

The gentle cat ignored his calls and continued to wander off. Peter followed him, hoping he wouldn't knock anything over.

"Rune...Come back here."

Following the willful white tiger, they found themselves in the middle of a modern art exhibit.

"This exhibit is rather extensive, isn't it, sir? Madam Cornhen handles all the pieces herself. Not many people in the manor are that familiar with Earth's art, though most find it fascinating," said Monty, as he pressed his nose up to a glass case housing a huge fist made up of thousands of red marbles. "Oh, look at Rune."

Peter spun and saw Rune gazing up curiously at a large, eclectic oil painting of a tiger in a suit and tie, reading the newspaper. The piece was titled, 'Paw Paws.'

"That is adorable!" said Madam Cornhen, "I wonder if Rune agrees with this depiction? Maybe some of his friends at the animal preserve would object! It's actually a rare piece. It's very expensive, due to... what's he doing?"

Peter's amusement vanished as Rune jumped up and pressed his two front paws against the painting, jostling its intricate golden frame.

"Rune!" yelled Peter, running over and gently nudging the heavy tiger. Rune obliged and reared back down to the floor. Madam Cornhen looked like she was about to faint. "It's okay Madam Cornhen, the canvas isn't marked!" he continued.

"It's...it's all right, Master Huddleston," she replied, her hand to her chest. "I would prefer, however, that Rune be escorted out of the museum, I don't think my heart could take it if something were destroyed."

"Of course, Madam Cornhen. I'm really sorry," said Peter, petting Rune, who continued to stare at the painting.

"I apologize, Madam Cornhen," stammered Ms. Homebody, "I should have asked you about bringing Rune; it's my fault."

"Jessica, dear, it's fine, really. No harm done," Madam Cornhen replied, the color returning to her face.

"Well..." Ms. Homebody started. "The painting is called, 'Paw Paws', maybe he thought they were instructions?" she said jokingly, a nervous smile forming on her face. "Get it? Paw paws! Because...hee hee...he's a cat, and...hee hee...HA HA HA HA HA..."

Peter noticed Madam Cornhen's eye start to twitch considerably.

Later that night, as he and Rune rested in his guarded and warded bedroom, Peter pondered all that had happened since he arrived at the manor. It had been a long and eventful summer, all he had to do was get through tomorrow, and Knor would have no basis to keep challenging Aunt Gillian's throne.

Everything depended on this last rite. He had to be ready. He had to pass it.

The next day, the council room was even more crowded than usual, as nobles and aristocrats of every caliber were there to witness Peter's fourth and final challenge. Gazing into the crowd, he was happy to see that even Mr. Frank, Ms. Homebody, Madam Cornhen and Ben were there, rooting him on with the rest of the enthusiastic assemblage. And, unless his eyes were failing him, he saw...yes, it was them! The Twickeypoos! His grandparents were in a middle row, beaming and waving at him with pride! He was stunned at how different they looked, both draped in light golden clothes and medaled sashes. He hardly recognized them. No wonder he couldn't find any pictures of them when he skimmed through his political science book! He waved happily back at them and had to control himself from running into the audience to greet them. To dampen the merriment, though, there was Knor, ever behind his podium, casting his dark shroud over everything.

Encouraged by the cheers, Peter apprehensively stepped into the glowing Pollana.

As the glow of the Pollana faded, Peter opened his eyes to a cavern of dark, crimson colored stone. He was stunned to feel how unbelievably hot it was. The heat and the size of the cavern made him think he was somehow inside a volcano. In front of him, several yards away, was what appeared to be an enormous, reddish-gray bird. As the giant bird screeched awfully, Peter saw a glint of gold. Looking more closely at the bird, Peter thought he saw scales covering its huge body. Its powerful wings beat wildly at Peter's presence. Looking past the monster, he saw that it was guarding the last scepter. "I don't believe this!" he said. "I'm supposed to take the scepter away from a dragon!"

Peter stood quietly in the darkened Pollana. The dragon slowly rose to its scaly feet. He noticed how old and feeble it looked, if dragons can be feeble. The mythic monster let out a piercing cry, and spread its massive wings into the humid air. Suddenly the entire cavern burst into flames. Everything except the area he was standing in, inside the Pollana, was completely consumed by crackling fire. He felt the intense heat on his skin. The dragon comfortably sat back down, engulfed in flame. This was his challenge, get through a raging inferno, defeat a dragon, and get the final scepter.

Peter looked around him. All he saw were the barren rock walls of the cavern, and he was completely surrounded by fire. He couldn't think of anything useful he could do with his boomerang, except maybe anger the creature further, and as far as he could see, the only good thing about this situation was that the beast wasn't attacking him.

He could see no tools or weapons in the cave, nothing to help him reach the scepter. He reached into his book bag for his Creamers box.

Peter had nine Creamers left, but he had no idea what any of them did. Four of them had different animals on each of their surfaces, a wolf, a hummingbird, a fish and a spider. The other five Creamers were each very different. One was decorated with a red cross; another had a fist; there was the Creamer in the middle with crossbones; one was shaped like a leaf, and one looked like a marshmallow. He had no idea which one to pick, and making matters worse, the intense heat was starting to affect his concentration. It was becoming harder to think clearly. Thankfully, he noticed, the Creamers were not melting, though the box was getting rather hot.

"Okay, the animals, a hummingbird...flying? The first Creamer I had already did that, besides, that won't really help much here. A wolf...no idea. A fish? Turning into a fish right now would probably not help. A spider...webs, sticking to walls...hot, burning walls, no." he said aloud, trying desperately to keep his thoughts together. The growing heat was starting to take its toll. The other Creamers didn't seem appropriate either. The only one he could think of was the marshmallow. It had nothing on it, so it had as good a chance as any. All he knew was that he had to make a decision quickly. He wanted to just be safe and take each chocolate every hour until he found one that helped him, but the heat was making him dose off. He was already out of breath. If he passed out, he'd lose the challenge. This Creamer had to work.

Without another thought, Peter tossed the marshmallow into his mouth. It tasted like cotton candy and dissolved almost instantly. He waited impatiently for something to happen, and something did.

Wiping the perspiration from his face, he noticed he had no hand! Looking down at his body, all he saw were his clothes and book bag; his arms were gone.

"Oh great!" he yelled, "I'm invisible!" The dragon gave no notice of his sudden change, but it didn't matter, as he still didn't know what to do. It did not take long before even his invisibility was marred. His body became tarnished with soot and ash produced by the dragon's fire. Breathing was becoming almost impossible. He was very dizzy.

"Think!" Peter yelled to himself, trying to stay awake. "Courage, this is the rite of courage..."

Then he had a thought. Slowly, he moved his hand closer to the fire...yes, it was hot! He darted his finger into the flames. They were real. Ouch. But he noticed that once his finger was out of the fire, it didn't hurt at all. He darted his entire hand into the flames and felt himself getting burned. But as soon as he pulled his hand back...it felt fine. There was no lingering pain at all.

"The flames don't burn!" he said to himself, "They hurt, but they don't burn!"

Peter realized what he was meant to do. Steadying his hand in the inferno, he felt his skin burning and yelled out in pain. And what about the dragon? What would he do to it if he even managed to make it there without blacking out? He had to make a choice now or he would fail. Before he knew it, he had hurled himself into the flames.

Peter started screaming in complete agony. He could feel his entire body being totally destroyed. He couldn't even see anymore, he just sprinted in the direction of the dragon until he ran right into it.

He felt the beast's cold scales, and...the pain was gone. He opened his eyes and saw the inferno had disappeared. Standing in front of him was the dragon. Only up close it didn't really look like a dragon. Peter was confused. The red scales weren't really scales at all; they were... feathers. He studied the giant bird, trying to figure out how to get to the scepter. Then, quite unexpectedly, there was an explosion of fire and light!

Peter picked himself off the floor of the cavern, shaking his head to clear the ringing from his ears. As his vision cleared, the giant bird had disappeared, and where it stood was a pile of ashes, and next to it, the scepter. And a baby bird!

"A phoenix!" Peter whispered in astonishment. The tiny bird looked innocently up at him, chirping loudly. He picked up the gold scepter as the glow from behind him further illuminated the baby creature. After taking a few steps towards the lighted Pollana, Peter heard a loud squawking and turned around just in time to see the little bird ignite once again. When the blaze died out, he saw it had grown to the size of a falcon. The feathery phoenix slowly lifted its head from the smoking ashes and looked him straight in the eyes.

The menacing look on this birds face was not good. Peter didn't move. He could feel the Pollana a few feet away. He turned and leaped into it as fast as he could, already hearing the sound of the phoenix's rustling feathers as it took to flight. He was above the portal, about to become submersed in its glow, when he felt a strong tug on the scepter. Refusing to let go, he grabbed onto it with both hands as he was pulled swiftly up into the air. Glancing up, he saw the phoenix's large talons wrapped tightly around the gold rod as it carried him higher and higher into the cavern.

"Let go you dumb bird!" he yelled.

Suddenly he felt another flash of intense heat and light, as a hail of ash clouded his senses. Peering up, he noticed the phoenix was five times its previous size. Only one huge talon gripped the golden stave. The impressive creature was hovering steadily in midair, effortlessly hanging on to its confused cargo.

"What?" asked Peter, looking around at the distant cave walls. "Now what am I supposed to do?"

It was only when Peter gazed down from their great altitude that he realized they were directly above the glowing Pollana.

"Oh, come on!" he exclaimed loudly. "Really? The walking through fire wasn't enough?"

He felt another, stronger flash of heat from above him. An ash cloud engulfed him before floating lazily down the cavern. The large phoenix was now a mature red dragon, rhythmically flapping its large, intimidating wings. The temperature around them grew noticeably hot, and beads of sweat formed a river down Peter's soot covered face.

"So...what? I'm supposed to let go and fall heroically into the light? What if I miss? What if..."

An intense flash blinded him, and far below, the cavern once again burst into flames. The heat and height were beginning to make him feel sick and dizzy. The dragon above him seemed to be having difficulty carrying his weight. As the two of them bobbed precariously in the air, there was another blinding flash, and Peter was falling helplessly down the cavern, still clutching onto the golden scepter. Everything was a haze of heat and light, when another flash burst in front of him. His fall was cut short with a startling jolt. He was dangling in the air, as the falcon-sized phoenix flew steadily upward.

"O-Okay, s-so...if I ask to stop this rite, I fail...but how could I win this? We're too high for me to let go," he said out loud. "The Pollana looks like a marble from up here!"

Closing his eyes, Peter concentrated as hard as he could. He didn't want to let go of one hand to look for a Creamer. He was scarcely able to hang on with both hands as it was. He knew Aunt Gillian would never plan to expose him to any real danger. He determined that the phoenix would not let him hit the ground. This challenge is all about overcoming fear. Just like the flames he ran through, though terrifying, he was not in mortal danger. He must trust his aunt; he had to.

"Fine!" he shouted. "If I have to fall, then I'll fall! But I need the scepter. How do I get this bird to let it go?"

As if on command, the phoenix released its steel grip on the stave. Peter felt himself once again falling terrifyingly into the abyss. He could hear his own shouts echoing in his ears, as the wind rushed startlingly against his face. Through his tearing eyes, he could see the Pollana growing larger...larger. His heart was pounding so hard in his chest he thought he'd pass out, until...

"AHHHHHHHHHHHH...what?" Peter exclaimed with surprise, as he felt a sudden jolt on the scepter and stopped plummeting. About twenty feet above the Pollana, the phoenix slowly transported Peter, hanging on for dear life, down towards its hazy glow. The graceful bird released the scepter, and Peter began to sink into the mesmerizing light. He trembled violently as great waves of relief spread through his exhausted body.

The Galadrian court materialized in front of him, and he held up the last scepter in his quivering hand. The court was silent, watching him intently. And then, as one, they jumped to their feet! He had done it! He had completed the last rite! Peter was shaking uncontrollably, could scarcely breathe, and was covered head to toe in ash and sweat... but he did it! The cheers and applause were deafening.

All in the court were happy, except for one.

"The successor has completed the fourth and final rite," said Aunt Gillian proudly, "and has returned to us bearing the Scepter of Courage! He has proven himself to us all! Knor of the House of Shadowray, it was you who insisted upon these challenges, it was you who assisted in the preparation for all the rites, and now, with us all, you have witnessed the successor triumph! Do you deny his success?"

Knor, stoic in his icy glare, remained perfectly composed. A moment of silence passed before he answered, his voice strong and clear.

"No, your Majesty."

"Are your claims questioning the successor's worthiness satisfied?"

"Yes...your Majesty."

"Do you, in front of the entire Galadrian court, the Supreme Council and myself, have any more objections to the successor that you would like to bring forth? If so, speak now."

"No, your Majesty."

"Then be silent, Knor of Shadowray, your accusations have all been heard and addressed."

A rumble of applause emanated from the court. Knor, his confidence unwavering, slowly stepped off the golden podium and unapologetically took his seat.

"And now," said Aunt Gillian triumphantly, "We shall proceed with the signing of the Lorna. Lord Grandon, if you would."

Lord Grandon walked up to Peter and took the scepter from his hand, placing it in the remaining space in the crystal ceremonial case next to the other three scepters. The councilman was carefully handed the Lorna by one of the other elders. Lord Grandon held up the glowing, golden orb in both hands and stood next to Peter. Aunt Gillian, beaming, handed her nephew a beautiful golden quill. As Peter signed his name on the Lorna in what looked like white light, he heard the court once again stand to its feet in appreciation.

Holding up the Lorna in both hands, Lord Grandon spoke, "People of the court of Galadria, it is my great honor to present to you, Her Royal Majesty, Queen Gillian Willowbrook of the Noble House of Willowbrook, and her nephew, son of Her Royal Highness, Patricia Willowbrook, and conqueror of the four Rites of Passage, His Royal Highness, Peter Willowbrook Huddleston, our undisputed crown prince!"

As the crowd burst into shouts of joy, Peter, now holding his aunt's hand, knew he would never forget this day, or this moment. He was covered in soot, had made a very powerful enemy, and had just signed away his future to a land he'd never seen.

He couldn't remember ever feeling so happy.

✳ ✳ ✳

Walking down the hall back to his room, Peter couldn't believe he'd done it. He was the official heir to the Galadrian throne! It felt like a huge weight was lifted off his shoulders.

As Monty, William and Rune listened, he could hardly contain his excitement.

"I can't believe it, Monty," said Peter. "Can you? They're done! The rites are done!"

"Yes sir! It must be quite a relief! We are all exceedingly proud! Now we'd better get you to your room quickly, you're blanketed in soot."

"Can you believe it, William?" asked Peter, "I can't...I'm done!"

"Yes, sir," said William seriously, "It is truly a momentous occasion."

"Everyone seemed really pleased," Peter continued, as they found themselves a few yards away from his room, "It was fun shaking everyone's hand as they stepped through the portal back to Galadria. Even the Twickeypoos were there!"

"Yes sir," said Monty excitedly, "Now, you'd better bathe and dress quickly, you're expected at the banquet in...What's that sound...no...William, behind us!" In a split second, Monty turned and pulled out a rectangular device from his coat pocket. "Sir, your room, now!" he shouted, when to Peter's surprise, he shot what looked like a beam of crackling electricity down the hall. "Now!" he repeated, firing again.

Peter peered down the hall and saw a dark figure racing towards them, narrowly evading Monty's attack.

"Go!" William shouted, pushing him towards his room as Monty fired three more consecutive blasts.

A dark, snake-like rope sped down the hall, wrapping itself around Monty's blaster and crushing it to pieces. As Monty reached for a secret button concealed in his belt, the dark rope mercilessly pummeled his head, sending him crashing to the floor.

"Monty!" yelled Peter, as his friend lay crumpled in front of him, "What's..."

Peter looked up to see what had hit Monty so violently on the head. It looked like a black pole was making its way from where Monty was laying to a cloaked figure walking straight towards them...Knor. He was holding the other end of the black pole, which Peter now recognized as a dark leeana, the same type of Protava Aunt Gillian had. Peter could hear William shouting at him, he could hear Rune, growling at his side, but all he could do was stare at Knor's sinister face. Knor had come here to destroy him, and Peter couldn't bring himself to move. He was frozen.

"YOUR ROOM, NOW!" shouted William, who literally picked Peter up and threw him towards the bedroom door. Peter landed about a foot in front of his room, turning to see William unsheathe his sword.

"But Monty's hurt, he..."

"GET IN YOUR ROOM AND CLOSE THE DOOR!" William yelled.

Peter saw Knor stride swiftly towards them. He bent his leeana effortlessly now, as if it were nothing more than rope. As Peter reached for the handle of his door, he saw Knor fling the dark rope at William. It wrapped and coiled itself around his sword, crushing and distorting its razor sharp edges as if they were clay. William leaped forward and struck out at Knor, pummeling his face with a barrage of heavy punches. Knor stumbled back, beckoning his dark leeana to his defense, as the dense rope hammered at William's armored chest. Rune positioned himself in front of Peter, growling fiercely. Peter pushed his door open, the motion caught Knor's eye. Seeing this, William tackled Knor, sending them both falling to the floor. Knor's leeana, despite William's distractive attack, made its way towards Peter like a menacing serpent. Peter and Rune rushed into his room and slammed the door shut, but it wouldn't close! Looking down, Peter saw Knor's indestructible rope edging its way up the frame, preventing the door from closing. Peter tried prying it off, but it was no use, he couldn't move it.

"CLOSE THE DO-UHHH!" came William's strangled voice from the hall. Peter heard Knor's shouts, as the Royal Guard smashed his head into the wall, trying to make him lose his hold on his Protava.

"William!" yelled Peter.

Suddenly the dark rope pulsed and the door was thrust open with such force that Peter was thrown to the floor. The rope wrapped itself painfully around his ankle and effortlessly dragged him out into the hall, before releasing him and re-launching itself at William.

"William, watch out!" yelled Peter, as he lay on the floor outside his door. As he yelled his warning, the tapestry on the wall next to him started emitting an eerie light, and a giant eagle flew out of it! The imposing beast beat its wings and began screeching wildly, launching its dagger sized talons at Knor! Peter saw William fall to the floor near Monty, clutching at his throat, desperately trying to breathe.

The leeana released its strangling grip from William's neck and snapped swiftly back to Knor. He began spinning it in front of him in a broad circular motion, forming a kind of shield. The giant eagle slashed relentlessly at Knor's makeshift defense with its great claws, its screeching deafening in the echoing hall. Peter could feel himself being pushed back, as the wind from its massively beating wings had the effect of a gale. The eagle's menacing barrage eventually started to break through. Knor's head suddenly jerked back, and blood trickled down a deep cut across his face. Then, from behind Knor, out of the shadows, Peter saw someone walking slowly towards them. The tall, slim silhouette crept closer and closer until it was right behind Knor and the giant eagle. Peter thought he was hallucinating...it was Madam Cornhen! She walked silently up behind Knor and started to unravel the coiled silver belt around her waist. Peter was filled with fear, if Knor turned around, he would surely kill her. Despite the savage onslaught of the giant eagle, Knor was unflinchingly standing his ground. Madam Cornhen, holding her long, bullwhip-like belt, raised her hand behind Knor's head, ready to strike at him. In one fluid motion, Knor...ducked. Peter, aghast, saw Knor slipping out of the way, as Madam Cornhen's silver belt whipped around the screeching eagle's thick neck!

"NOW VIVIAN!" yelled Knor. His leeana shot from his hand and coiled itself around the great eagle's massive wings. Straining, Madam Cornhen jerked her silver whip sending the huge beast falling to the floor. Already, Knor's coiled leeana was unraveling against the creature's considerable strength. Knor unsheathed a gleaming sword from his robes, and to Peter's horror, stood over the screeching eagle and brutally hacked at its neck. The first few blows seemed to go unnoticed, as the creature continued to bite at Knor, sending blood spraying from his hand. Knor persisted in his attack, putting all his weight and strength into each successive blow. Just as the giant's thrashing freed its wings from the dark leeana, it's head flipped awkwardly back. There was a flash of light, and the giant eagle burst into an explosion of feathers. The shredded, hanging tapestry fell heavily to the floor. Madam Cornhen held fast onto her whip, while Knor's leeana slithered quickly back into his hands. Peter leaped into his room.

"AHHHH!" Peter yelled, as he felt a sharp pain on his leg and was sent crashing to the floor. In one violent tug, he was pulled back out into the hall. Looking down, he saw Madam Cornhen's silver whip wrapped around his calf.

"M-Madam Cornhen," said Peter, shocked, "Why...Why are you..."

"Why am I what?" she said in a cold, cruel voice, her sweet disposition gone to reveal a face full of malice. "Why am I here to help kill you? Why am I here to see my cousin take his rightful place on the throne? Why am I here to assure my family takes an unparalleled place in history? I'll tell you why, because I'd rather die than bow down to another Willowbrook!"

"Your cousin? Knor's your..."

"Yes, you ignorant little infant." said Knor sharply, "My beloved cousin, Vivian Shadowray. She's had to stay at this vile, putrid estate for years to spy for our family. I've waited far too long for the right time to challenge Gillian's throne, and when I do...you appear. Just a child, I told myself, and not even a capable one at that. I was certain the rites would eliminate you, but the council was too lenient. Twice, while I was undoubtedly with the council elders, Vivian risked exposing her identity to come here to finish you...but this damn door! I owe it to her to let her see you die."

Suddenly, Rune, fangs bared and emitting a deadly growl, stepped menacingly towards Knor. Knor raised his leeana into the air...

"Let me, Knor," said Madam Cornhen, as she took his sword from him, "I have a score to settle with that beast, he almost discovered the portal."

"The Portal?" Peter whispered, "But the only time you were with Rune outside the study room was...the tiger painting! Paw Paws!"

"Not as dim as you look, you little runt," said Madam Cornhen coldly, "I've spent years secretly building that portal, and that obnoxious cat almost exposed everything! It will be a pleasure to eliminate him!"

As Madam Cornhen raised her hand high into the air, her silver whip uncoiled from Peter's leg. Knor too, prepared to strike.

Thoughts raced through Peter's head...they were going to kill him... then they would dispose of Rune. What about the rest of the manor? The Twickeypoos, Aunt Gillian...Peter had to make a choice. It was the same feeling he got when he accepted Aunt Gillian's proposal to be her successor, the same feeling he got before each Rite of Passage. He did not get this far only to have it end like this. He was not going to let Knor hurt his family. He was not going to give up.

Peter could feel his mind going blank. He let the numbness overcome his fear. Grabbing his boomerang from his pocket, he jumped to his feet.

"You two want to kill me, Knor?" he said, his own voice now sharp and sure. "Take your best shot."

"Kill the tiger Vivian, leave the boy to me."

As if on cue, Rune leaped forward, claws bared, as Madam Cornhen started whipping at him savagely. Knor advanced on Peter, his leeana now forming a solid staff. Peter threw his boomerang as hard as he could at Knor's head, but Knor blocked it swiftly with his dark staff. Peter threw it again and again, but Knor kept blocking it. Peter threw it as fast as he could, catching the boomerang over and over again as he hailed it at Knor's face. The boomerang flew back and forth so fast it looked like a continuous motion of movement, a constant blur, until finally... one connected! Knor's head jerked back as Peter's boomerang hit him straight on. But Peter did not relent. Seeing he had broken through, he threw his boomerang even harder and faster at Knor, hitting him again and again. Finally, anchoring himself, Knor once again began to block Peter's attack, and lunged at him with his leeana staff. Peter couldn't believe it. He had hit Knor over a half dozen times head on and it hadn't even fazed him. Knor took a deadly swing with his staff, and Peter barely blocked it, deflecting it away with his indestructible boomerang. Then, holding both ends of his boomerang, he thrust its face as hard as he could against Knor's head, making him stumble backwards.

"You vermin!" said Knor fiercely, his hand to his head.

Behind Knor, Peter thought he saw Monty stirring, his head turning on the ground. He could see Madam Cornhen whipping at Rune, trying to get her whip around his neck like she did with the eagle. With the gleaming sword in her other hand she slashed at Rune's bared fangs. In one motion, she managed to get her whip around Rune's neck, as she pulled in closer and advanced with the sword.

"Die, cat!" she shrieked.

Peter threw his boomerang at Knor, who ducked out of the way, but as Peter had intended, it hit Madam Cornhen and made her stagger back. With his staff raised to attack, Knor stood back up...directly into the path of Peter's boomerang. The boomerang sped back from striking Madam Cornhen and whacked the back of Knor's head before landing safely in Peter's hand.

"ENOUGH!" snarled Knor. He whipped his dark leeana around Peter's arm. With one powerful push from his dark protava, Knor catapulted Peter into the air and sent him crashing against the wall behind him. Peter bounced off the wall and hit the floor hard.

"EEHHHH...that...wasn't...so...bad..." gasped Peter, his voice forced out between shallow breaths. The force of Knor's attack had all but knocked him out. He was sure some of his ribs were broken. Gathering his remaining strength, Peter heaved his boomerang at Knor's head... and missed. His desperate throw embedded his Protava into the wall.

"Your minimal talent is fading," sneared Knor. "Now you don't even have that stupid toy to protect...UHHH!"

Peter reached out his hand and caught his returning boomerang. Taking advantage of Knor's surprise, he braced himself against the wall and kicked Knor in the stomach. As Knor fell back, Peter got up and ran down the hall, reaching blindly into his book bag. Knor whipped his leeana at him and caught him around the ankles, sending him tumbling to the floor as his Creamers sprayed out in front of him.

"No!" yelled Knor, as he dragged Peter towards him. "Just like a Willowbrook to rely on tricks to make up for their weakness!"

Peter reached out and grabbed the first Creamer he could get his hands on. As he stuffed it into his mouth, he saw it was the one marked with the fist.

Knor, his leeana now a staff, was about to strike...when Peter felt different. Out of nowhere he leaped to his feet, and with all his might, punched Knor as hard as he could, sending him flying backwards, smashing into the wall behind him. Peter felt like he had the strength of ten men!

"How do you like that trick, Knor?"

Knor rose to his feet, his leeana now a dark rope in his hands. He started spinning the rope in front of him before it shot out and coiled itself around Peter's neck.

"You've wasted enough of my time, child! Consider yourself privileged, you will be known as the Willowbrook whose death made me a king!" said Knor triumphantly, holding fast to the other end of his leeana.

It was like being strangled by a thick, steel cable. Peter couldn't breathe. He knew he would black out in a matter of seconds.

Grabbing the length of rope in front of him, Peter pulled it as hard as he could and swung it towards the wall behind him, sending Knor smashing against it and falling heavily to the floor...but he still didn't let go.

"I will admit...a good effort, boy," Knor said, winded. He slowly stood up and continued to control his constricting leeana. "But what made you think you had a chance against a nobleman of Shadowray?"

Peter dropped to the floor; he felt his life being squeezed out of him. His vision blurring, he could see Rune still fighting off Madam Cornhen. Then, in a haze, he thought he saw her fall to the floor. Looking up, Peter saw Knor standing over him, smiling cruelly as he gasped for breath. Without warning, behind Knor's shoulder, he could just make out a shimmer...of gold.

Knor was pulled back as a golden rope wrapped itself around his neck. Peter gasped for air as he felt the force of Knor's leeana release.

There was a loud crash as Knor was hurled against the wall. Peter could dimly make out Aunt Gillian and over a dozen armed guards standing behind her, seven of them in golden armor with swords and shields in hand. Rune was at her side, fangs and claws bared. Knor got to his feet and commanded his dark leeana into his hand.

Aunt Gillian, her golden rope twisting in her hands, focused on Knor.

"You take one step towards Peter," she said, her eyes locked in a deadly glare, "And I swear on my life Knor, I will kill you myself."

Peter saw Knor and Aunt Gillian standing defiantly across from each other, Knor seeming to weigh the situation.

In an instant, he hurled his leeana at Aunt Gillian's neck, as her own leeana flew impossibly from her hands. The Protavas coiled in midair before each being violently thrown back to its wielders ready grasp.

Peter saw as the guards watched, awestruck at the ensuing struggle, unsure of whether their monarch needed or even wanted their assistance.

Aunt Gillian's leeana shot out like a golden blur, circling in the air as it hit Knor over and over again across the side of his head.

For the first time, Peter saw Knor truly stagger, struggling to keep control of his own weapon as the golden barrage beat him into unconsciousness.

Peter watched in horror as Knor's dark rope slithered across the floor and wrapped itself around Aunt Gillian's legs, sending her tumbling down and dragging her towards him.

At once, the guards rushed in, but not before Rune, with a deafening roar, leaped into the air towards Knor's neck. Peter was amazed at the speed Knor's leeana released his aunt and wrapped itself around Rune's head, snapping shut his bared fangs only inches from his exposed throat. Rune managed to gash Knor's chest with his claws, before being hurled backwards into the troop of guards, knocking half of them heavily off their feet.

"Knor!" yelled Aunt Gillian, lithely jumping to her feet. "You will stop! NOW!"

In the next second, Knor was catapulted through the air. The golden rope was wrapped around his ankles, sending him crashing head first into the walls, again, and again, and again. Blood oozed from his head as he lay crumpled on the floor, but his dark rope managed to break Aunt Gillian's golden hold on his ankles.

Knor stumbled to his feet, a crazed and manic look emanating from his bloodied face.

"This is not over Gillian," he snarled, "Your family has horded power long enough! I vow the House of Shadowray will take your place! I WILL RULE GALADRIA, AND I WILL SEE YOU ALL DEAD!"

Knor quickly leaped to his side into Peter's bedroom, the door slamming shut behind him.

"Get him!" yelled Aunt Gillian, as her guards rushed the door.

"Your Majesty, the door's sealed itself! We cannot break through."

"Half of you to the gardens outside, the room's windows are the only other way out," said Aunt Gillian, as she ran and knelt at Peter's side. "Peter...Peter, can you hear me?"

"Aunt Gillian," Peter gasped, "He...he's going to the art exhibit...the museum...the tiger painting...Paw Paws...it's the portal...it's..."

"Peter..."

Peter could hear Aunt Gillian saying his name, he could feel Rune's soft fur beside him; he heard the steps of the guards as they rushed passed him to get to the gardens... then all he saw was darkness...

✳ ✳ ✳

"Peter...Peter..."

"Hmmmm?"

"You're awake!"

"Nuh-uh..." Peter groggily replied, as he felt someone's hand on his forehead. He reluctantly opened his eyes and saw Aunt Gillian staring back at him.

"Aunt Gillian..."

"It's alright, we..."

"Knor!" Peter yelled, as he sat bolt upright. His body ached horribly. Looking around, he saw he was in his bed, and as he felt his stinging ribs, he found they had been tightly bandaged. Aunt Gillian was sitting next to him.

"Peter, it's alright," she said soothingly, "You're safe now, you've been asleep for days.

"But what about Knor? Did you get him?"

"Calm down, I'll tell you everything that's happened.

We heard what you said about the portal, but he still managed to escape. Peter, breathe...okay, good. We raced him back to the art exhibit at the museum, our guards tried to stop him, but he fought them off. We weren't sure exactly which painting he was headed to, but when our guards saw the tiger portrait, they did everything they could to stop him from reaching it. He was barely able to fling his injured body into the portal. When our guards tried to follow, they couldn't get through. It must have instantly closed on the other side. Someone else must have been waiting for him for it to shut off that quickly."

"Oh...wait! But Madam Cornhen, she..."

"She's been arrested and is in Galadria awaiting trial. We were all shocked to find she was Knor's cousin. The House of Shadowray has never been honest with the rest of the noble families, but even then, we thought we at least knew who all of them were. Madam Cornhen, or rather Vivian Shadowray, has been working here for years. We hired her in Galadria and did an extensive background check but never found anything connecting her with Shadowray. We suspect their entire clan was involved in concealing her identity."

"Did she make the portal?" Peter asked wearily.

"She confessed to bringing back tiny, concealed pieces of the portal with her every time she returned from Galadria." she continued. "It must have taken years for her to get it all here. Then, when she was suppose to be restoring the museum's older paintings in her restoration studio, she was secretly building the portal onto the back of the tiger painting's heavy frame. When we inspected the frame, we were amazed at the intricacy of her work. Very few specialized engineers are skilled enough to build portals. I've never seen one that thin and streamlined before. Every portal I've used is quite large and bulky. It's no wonder it was overlooked when the manor was searched. It never occurred to us a portal could be built that small. It was amazing she did it on her own. The canvas was even easily detachable to allow the traveler to step through the frame. She and Knor had left the gateway on. When he dove into the portal to flee the guards, the painting was pushed in with him."

"I still can't believe Madam Cornhen was a Shadowray spy!" he exclaimed, "Twichie-eyed, Zvella dessert loving, Madam Cornhen!"

"I know. It's shocking. I'm still surprised we weren't completely invaded. Apparently she only finished building the portal recently. Maybe the Shadowrays found her too useful as a spy to expose her and what she had built here," she offered, "Knor must have just planned to dispose of you, then return back through the portal undetected. It was a desperate act.

"Madam Cornhen was the one who tried to attack you when you were alone in your room both those times, but she couldn't defeat the Danjanestry by herself. We couldn't believe what she had done, many in this manor thought of her as a good friend. Poor Ms. Homebody fainted when she found out that she had attacked you."

"But where's Knor now?"

"We suspect somewhere in Galadria. His portal here in the manor was destroyed. After we had our engineers inspect it, they couldn't determine precisely where it led. Under royal command, we searched the House of Shadowray from top to bottom and couldn't find him or the other end of the illegal portal. They've all been told that contact with him is forbidden, and that if any of them help him they'd be arrested immediately. The entire court and Supreme Council have been informed and were completely outraged. Many of the noble families took it upon themselves to organize search parties for Knor throughout Galadria. He is to be arrested on sight. Everyone in Galadria knows what happened and is looking for him. Knor was unpopular before, but now he'll really be hunted.

"Won't he come after me?"

"I don't think he can. From the guards report, he was almost killed in his clash with them. He barely escaped. His portal to Hillside is gone.

The entire mansion is being searched again for anything that might have been transported through the secret portal. We are literally taking the museum apart and all the other paintings are being inspected. All the Shadowrays are under surveillance and literally everyone is looking for him. His political career is over. If he comes out of hiding and shows his face anywhere, he'll be signing his own death warrant. It's only a matter of time before he's found...oh, before I forget...you wouldn't want to lose this."

Aunt Gillian lifted Peter's leather book bag up next to him, he peered inside to see everything in place, including his boomerang. Reaching in and pulling out his polished wooden box, he opened it to see his seven remaining Creamers perfectly intact.

"Aunt Gillian, how did you know to come help us?"

"Monty came running to tell us what was happening. How he made it that far with that bump on his head I'll never know."

"Monty...MONTY!" cried Peter suddenly, just noticing him standing quietly in the corner of the room. "Are you okay?"

"Yes, sir," said Monty, smiling down at him, "Still have a bit of a headache, but other than that...you had us worried, sir."

"Oh I'm alright, I...WILLIAM! Is he...?"

"He's fine," said Aunt Gillian, "He's been asking about you. William, could you come in please."

The door opened and William entered in his shining golden armor. Upon seeing Peter awake, he broke out in a huge smile.

"It is a blessing to see you up, Master Huddleston,"

"William! You...thank you...you...my life...all of you!" Peter said.

"Rune!" Peter cried as the purring tiger pounced up on the bed and nuzzled into him. "I didn't see...Monty, Aunt Gillian, Rune...you saved my...my..."

"Alright Peter, don't get too excited, you're still not fully recovered," said his aunt, as Peter started to feel very dizzy.

"The eagle, they killed it...it exploded...feathers everywhere..."

"Relax," she continued, "The Danjanestry is already being repaired, it's quite a job, but once all the feathers are woven back into the tapestry it will be fine."

"But...but..."

"Here," she said, taking a rather large, golden bowl from Monty, "Have some honey tea, I'm sure you need it."

Peter slowly sat up and started drinking the hot tea. He felt his body strengthen.

"Peter..." continued Aunt Gillian, "I just want you to know...I'm so sorry this happened. You fought so bravely, and against someone like Knor. He...he could have..."

"It's okay," he said consolingly, seeing the look on his aunt's face. "No one knew what would happen. I saw you fight him. You risked your life for me. I've never had anyone really stick up for me before, and what you all did, putting yourselves in danger...I'll never forget that."

✳ ✳ ✳

The next few days passed rather uneventfully. Peter spent most of his time resting comfortably in bed with Aunt Gillian constantly by his side. Monty made sure he was always full to bursting with honey tea, and after awhile, it worked! With astonishing quickness, Peter was out of bed and walking around his room. Monty would bring them their meals, and as aunt and nephew ate, laughing and chatting, Rune would curl up beside them, purring contentedly.

12

BACK TO BEIGE

The rest of Peter's time at Hillside Manor felt oddly bittersweet. The summer was drawing to a close and soon he knew he would have to leave. He had already finished his last few classes and had expressed to Mr. Frank, Ms. Homebody, Ben and William how much their time meant to him, and how much he appreciated all their efforts.

"THANK YOU SO MUCH FOR YOUR LESSONS, MR. FRANK." Peter said, as Ms. Homebody, Monty and Ben looked on.

"You're welcome, Master Huddleston, I expect to see you bright and ready next year."

"YOU WILL, SIR."

"Good, good," said Mr. Frank, as they shook hands.

"You best keep practicing with your boomerang there, keep doing those tricks we worked on." Ben added, smiling, "Never know when they'll come in handy, eh?"

"Will do," Peter replied, "Take care of Rune for me, okay? Uh, watch out for those hippos too."

"Sure thing."

"Ms. Homebody, thanks for..." Peter started, but...

"Master Huddleston, it has been such a pleasure, an absolute pleasure! Remember, study hard and no matter what's happened, always think happy thoughts! Oh! I almost forgot," she said, reaching into her bag, "Mother made you a tin of chocolate chip cookies, she sends her best."

"Thanks," said Peter, taking the decorated tin, "Thank her for me."

"She'll be thrilled, really! I can't believe you're...you're... WAAAAAA!"

To everyone's surprise, out of nowhere, perennially cheerful Ms. Homebody had burst into tears.

"Don't cry Ms. Homebody, I'll see you next..."

"I know, I know," she said, dabbing at her tear filled eyes, "it's just...I just...WAAAAAAAA! Oh, Montgomery, hold me!"

"Jessica, I don't think it would be appropriate to..."

"I SAID HOLD ME!"

"Oh, all right!" said Monty, putting his arm around her.

Peter also got to see the Twickeypoos, and had a very nice lunch with them before they had to return to their sweet shop. He thanked them profusely for his special Creamers, and knowing they would see each other very soon, he said his farewells to them, not as 'Mr. and Mrs. Twickeypoo,' but as 'Grandma and Grandpa.'

The night before his father was set to pick him up, Peter had a private dinner with Aunt Gillian and Rune in one of the more intimate state dining rooms. They dined on fresh Galadrian pears, as was custom for a farewell dinner, as well as various Galadrian cheeses, meats and of course, chocolates.

"I've already spoken to your father on the phone," said Aunt Gillian sweetly, "He promised to bring you back next summer."

"I guess I shouldn't mention any of what's happened, huh?"

"I think it would be best, at least for now."

"I don't want to leave at all," said Peter, truthfully.

"I don't want to see you go either, but you need to finish school and be with your father. He needs you. Just know this is your home. Without you, our family at Hillside just isn't complete."

"Thanks, Aunt Gillian."

"Don't forget, Rune will miss you too," she said, turning to the purring tiger sprawled out on the floor, chewing an enormous, juicy steak.

That night, as Monty walked him to his room, Peter noticed he was more quiet than usual.

"You alright, Monty?"

"Oh yes, sir, I just... I...WAAAAAA..."

The next thing Peter knew, Monty had flung his arms around him and was sobbing uncontrollably.

"I-I'll see you next summer," said Peter, taken aback by this dramatic show of emotion. Monty was squeezing him so tightly he could hardly breathe.

"Monty...Monty, too tight, too tight..." he gasped, through shallow breaths.

"W-what? Oh y-yes sir, so sorry...don't know what came over me," said Monty, regaining his composure and releasing a teetering Peter. "Silly of me really," he continued, pulling out a large, striped blue handkerchief and blowing his nose loudly.

Peter could have sworn Rune was laughing.

The next day, Peter found himself in front of the high arched doors at the entrance of the manor, standing on the same familiar cream-colored steps, waiting for his father to arrive. Aunt Gillian, Monty, Mrs. Smith and Rune were all gathered around to see him off.

The manor's huge gray gates slowly opened as a little beige car drove confidently up to them. To Peter's surprise, his dad hopped quickly out of the car and hugged him, albeit for half a second.

"Good to see you," said his father sincerely.

"You too, Dad,"

"Have you had a good sum..." he started, but Peter noticed the sight of Aunt Gillian had distracted him. "Hello, Gillian."

"Hello Andrew," she said, kindly, "It's been far too long."

"Y-yes...thank you for taking care of Peter."

"It was truly our pleasure, we can't wait to see him again."

"Well we...is...is that a tiger!"

"This is Rune, Dad," he said casually, gingerly patting the furry tiger's head.

"We...uh...we better get going," Andrew continued, completely taken aback by the white tiger licking his hand.

"Bye Monty, bye Mrs. Smith," Peter called out, waving to both of them at the top of the steps. "Bye Rune," he continued, when to his father's horror, he knelt down and hugged the gentle cat.

Peter went to his aunt and gave her one final hug.

"I love you, Peter," she whispered.

"I love you too," he said quietly back.

And in a few moments, Peter was in the beige car, waving goodbye to his newfound family.

"Did you have a good time?"

"The best time, Dad." he said happily.

"Does Gillian always wear gowns like that?"

"Always," he replied, a smile forming on his face.

"Three more days on the road, I'm not sure if I can remember how to get home."

Taking a deep breath, Peter took one final look at the manor wall behind them. A sense of calm came over him. He felt...complete.

"Don't worry Dad...we'll find our way."

ABOUT THE AUTHOR:

Miguel Lopez de Leon is a novelist who lives in Los Angeles and is the author of the "Galadria" fantasy book trilogy. Book 1, "Galadria: Peter Huddleston & The Rites of Passage" is the first book of the series, followed by Book 2, "Galadria: Peter Huddleston & The Mists of the Three Lakes," and Book 3, "Galadria: Peter Huddleston & The Knights of the Leaf."

Miguel's latest fantasy books are "The Unicorn," "Carry the Knight," and it's sequel, "Dawn of the Knight."

Prior to his novels, Miguel was an accomplished short story writer, even winning first place in Writer's Digest Magazine's "Your Story # 24" writing contest. His short story, "A Working Professional," beat out over 550 other competitors in the international contest.

Miguel's various short stories were published in The Shine Journal, The Oddville Press Magazine, The Cynic Magazine, Fantastic Horror Magazine, The Absent Willow Review, Hungur Magazine, Illumen Digest, Sounds of the Night Magazine, Niteblade Magazine, The Solid Gold Anthology- UK (Published by Gold Dust Magazine), The Cover of Darkness Anthology, as well as seven separate paperback anthologies by Pill Hill Press.

Aside from writing, Miguel's other interests include the real estate business, financial investing, and philanthropic work with several international organizations.

Miguel has also modeled for various international brands, such as Diesel, and was chosen as the main face for a print ad campaign for the Italian brand "Bergamo."

For more info. go to www.miguellopezdeleon.com